Dear Reader,

I believe when most folks think of Texas they conjure up the image of the Great Plains, cowboys, horses and cattle, oil wells and businessmen, the Alamo and NASA. Sometimes it's forgotten that Texas also has hundreds of miles of beautiful coastline with wide sandy beaches and hot, hot sun.

When I first saw Galveston Island, I wasn't a Texan. I lived in the Oklahoma hills where the only large bodies of water were freshwater lakes. Needless to say, I was enchanted with the Gulf of Mexico and decided then and there that I had to write a romance set on the island—a fun, laid-back story that would depict life on the Texas Coast. The result was *Precious Pretender*.

At the time, I would have never guessed that years later my husband and I, along with our son, would be moving to Texas to a tiny town on the coast where shrimping and cattle ranching go hand in hand.

The Lone Star State will always have a special mystique about it and thankfully, for all of us, there will always be romances written about Texans. I hope you enjoy reading my contribution, *Precious Pretender*. If you're not a Texan, come visit us sometime. And if you already live down here in this wonderful state, then I'll just "Howdy, neighbor!"

Love and God Bless,

GREATEST TEXAS LOVE STORIES OF ALL TIME

GREATEST

TEXAS LOVE STORIES
OF ALL TIME

PRECIOUS PRETENDER
Stella Bagwell

Heading to the Hitchin' Post

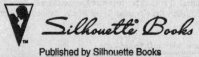

Published by Silhouette Books
America's Publisher of Contemporary Romance

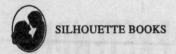

SILHOUETTE BOOKS

ISBN 0-373-65216-X

PRECIOUS PRETENDER

Copyright © 1991 by Stella Bagwell

Printed in U.S.A.

STELLA BAGWELL

sold her first book to Silhouette in November 1985. More than forty novels later, she still loves her job and she says she isn't completely content unless she's writing. Recently she and her husband of thirty years moved from the hills of Oklahoma to Seadrift, Texas, a sleepy little fishing town located on the coastal bend. Stella says the water, the tropical climate and the seabirds make it a lovely place to let her imagination soar and to put the stories in her head down on paper.

She and her husband have one son, Jason, who lives and teaches high school math in nearby Port Lavaca.

Books by Stella Bagwell

Silhouette Romance

Golden Glory #469
Moonlight Bandit #485
A Mist on the Mountain #510
Madeline's Song #543
The Outsider #560
The New Kid in Town #587
Cactus Rose #621
Hillbilly Heart #634
Teach Me #657
The White Night #674
No Horsing Around #699
That Southern Touch #723
Gentle as a Lamb #748
A Practical Man #789
Precious Pretender #812
Done to Perfection #836
Rodeo Rider #878
*Their First Thanksgiving #903
*The Best Christmas Ever #909

*New Year's Baby #915
Hero in Disguise #954
Corporate Cowgirl #991
Daniel's Daddy #1020
A Cowboy for Christmas #1052
Daddy Lessons #1085
Wanted: Wife #1140
†The Sheriff's Son #1218
†The Rancher's Bride #1224
†The Tycoon's Tots #1228
†The Rancher's Blessed Event #1296
†The Ranger and the Widow Woman #1314
†The Cowboy and the Debutante #1334
†Millionaire on Her Doorstep #1368
The Bridal Bargain #1414
Falling for Grace #1456
The Expectant Princess #1504
The Missing Maitland #1546
Because of the Ring #1589

Silhouette Special Edition

Found: One Runaway Bride #1049
†Penny Parker's Pregnant! #1258
White Dove's Promise #1478

**Heartland Holidays
†Twins on the Doorstep

Silhouette Books

The Fortunes of Texas
The Heiress and the Sheriff

Maitland Maternity
Just for Christmas

A Bouquet of Babies
"Baby on Her Doorstep"

Midnight Clear
†"Twins under the Tree"

Going to the Chapel
"The Bride's Big Adventure"

To my sister, Thelma, and those crazy situations
we somehow manage to get ourselves into.
You've taught me a lot, sis, and I love you dearly.

Chapter One

"Priscilla, what are you doing in bed? It's only eleven!"

Priscilla's groan was muffled by the pillows. Then she slowly turned her head and cracked open one eye at the strip of light slanting across the end of her bed. "Damn it, Rick, I told you to stay out of my diet sodas! And why are you waking me at this hour?"

Rick's deep laugh preceded his tall form in the doorway. "Priscilla, you're getting stuffier every day. The night is just beginning. There's a full moon hanging over the ocean and you're in bed wasting it."

Priscilla clamped her eyes shut as he flipped on the overhead light. "Turn that out! And if it's so wonderful out there, why aren't you there instead of here in my bedroom. I thought you had a date.''

Ignoring her order to switch off the light, Rick lazily propped one broad shoulder against the door-jamb. ''I did, but Angie and I had a blowup so I took her home—for good.''

And now he was here—where he always was after he'd broken up with one of his endless string of girlfriends. She opened one eye and watched him tilt the aluminum can to his lips. ''You owe me seven cans of root beer,'' she told him, ''and that's only counting this week's.''

He swallowed down half the can before lowering it. Priscilla scowled as he looked at her and grinned rakishly. ''I'll bring them home from work tomorrow.''

Priscilla's snort was proof of how much faith she had in his promises. ''You said that two days ago.''

''So I forgot,'' he told her, moving into the room and taking a seat on the foot of the bed.

Rick had made himself at home in her apartment for the past year and a half, ever since he'd leased the other half of the beach house that had been converted into a duplex. By now Priscilla was very used to his comings and goings.

''Aren't you going to ask about Angie?'' he asked Priscilla.

Since he obviously wasn't going to go away,

Priscilla scooted up in the bed and propped her back against the brass bedstead. "Not really," she said, pushing her tousled brown hair back off her forehead.

Mock hurt wrinkled his handsome features. "But don't you want to know why we broke up?"

"Not really," she repeated with a hint of laughter in her voice. Rick's eyes lowered to her T-shirt with Mickey Mouse plastered across the front. One corner of his mouth lifted with amusement.

Seeing it, Priscilla asked sharply, "What's so funny?"

He nodded toward the outline of her ample bust. "You've got Mickey's ears bent out of shape. The poor guy must be in pain."

Priscilla glared at him. "Would you mind taking yourself off to your own bed? I'd like to make use of this one."

"Yes, I would mind," he retorted. "I'm not through with my drink and I haven't told you about Angie yet. Besides," he said, stretching out across the foot of the bed, and propping his head up on one bent elbow, "your bed feels better than mine."

Priscilla rolled her eyes. "That's because I saved my money and bought a new mattress. Unlike someone else I know."

Laughing under his breath, Rick rolled to his back and balanced the can of root beer upon his midsection. Priscilla looked at him, thinking how shocked her co-workers would be if they could see her now, wearing nothing but a T-shirt, with Rick lazily planted on the foot of the bed.

Rick was a gorgeous man. Priscilla supposed that was one reason why she'd never felt threatened by him. With his dark blond hair, sky blue eyes and a body like a running back's, women were drawn to him like moths to a light bulb. And since Priscilla was just a plain little cricket in the dark, there was never a danger in allowing Rick on her bed.

"It was a tie," he said quietly, then suddenly he began to laugh deep in his throat, causing the aluminum can to teeter precariously. "I didn't have the graciousness to wear a tie to meet her mother."

Priscilla looked at him, a tiny frown marring her forehead. "Well, that's not as bad as the one who insisted you buy a new car before she'd go to dinner with you."

"Hmm, yeah. That was Liz. She had classy taste—for a while."

"You mean until she dropped you," Priscilla said with a yawn. "Rick, I can't understand this thing you have with women. You pick some of the most selfish, spoiled—"

"I know. It's the only weak trait I have." He rolled his head to one side, letting his eyes travel over Priscilla. "But at least I'm not afraid of having a little fun. Like someone else I know," he added suggestively.

"Fun! Rick, you're thirty years old! It's past time for you to grow up." She shot him a reproving look. "Get out of here. I have to get my sleep. Since tomorrow is Saturday, I've promised to help show an animal film to preschoolers at the library in the morning. So I have to get there early to help organize things."

Rick suddenly sat bolt upright. "Priscilla, are you sure an outing like that won't be too much excitement for you?"

She drew up her legs, then let them fly straight at him. Laughing, Rick slid lithely off the bed, out of reach of her feet.

"I can see I'm not going to get any sympathy out of you. I'm going to bed." He walked up to the head of the bed, then leaned down and pecked a kiss on her cheek. "Thanks for the root beer, darlin'. See you tomorrow."

"I didn't give you the root beer, Rick. You took it."

Grinning, he started out the door. "But you don't mind. Good night, Pris."

He turned off the light and Priscilla slid back down in the bed. "Good night, Rick," she said, pulling the sheet up over her shoulder.

She could hear his steps going back through the kitchen, then saw the light go out. There was a door between her refrigerator and electric range, which opened into Rick's identical kitchen. She heard it open, then close.

The door had always remained locked when past boarders had lived next to Priscilla. But, then, John and Martha Granger had kept to themselves. She'd hardly known they were there. But Rick was altogether different. In more ways than one.

Sighing, she rolled over to her side and gazed out the window. Since the blinds were raised, she could see that Rick had been telling the truth. A beautiful yellow moon hung out over the ocean and Galveston Island.

The sight of it brought a wistful expression to her face, and after a few moments she got out of bed and slipped on a pair of shorts and leather thongs. The early June night was warm, and the stiff ocean breeze whipped her brown hair away from her face as she walked down the outside stairs of the beach house.

Rick was wrong about her, she decided as she walked across the warm sand. She wasn't stuffy. Even if she looked plain and lived rather conventionally, she wasn't stuffy. She was going to remind him of that tomorrow.

Priscilla had left the small east-Texas town where she'd been born and had lived for twenty years to attend college and get her degree in elementary education. Everyone back in Jefferson had thought she would come back after college and make her home there. But she'd surprised them all, including her family, when she'd chosen to make her home on Galveston Island.

It had taken courage for Priscilla to make that decision. She'd always been guided and cared for by her parents, who thought of her as the bookish daughter. Her older sister Tracie was the beautiful, talented one.

Priscilla sat down on the damp sand, just close enough to allow the surf to lap over her toes. She didn't know why she was in such a pensive mood. If Rick hadn't woken her, she'd have been fast asleep by now. And what made him think she'd be interested to hear that he'd dropped Angie, she wondered with disgust.

The truth was she was getting tired of hearing about his girlfriends. Blondes, brunettes, redheads. She watched them come and go like a parade of high-bred horses. It angered her that he couldn't see through their shallowness.

Rick was a wonderful man, even if he had a flaw about women. He was witty and charming, and she'd learned over the past that he also had an intelligent mind to go with his looks. He worked for a marketing firm in Houston that dealt with petroleum. She'd asked him once exactly what he did do and laughing he'd said he talked on the phone, pushed the button on his desk intercom and signed his name to papers he never read.

She hadn't believed him. At least not entirely, and had pressed him to elaborate. So after a lengthy explanation from Rick she'd learned that he found dealers from all over the world to buy both raw and refined petroleum from Petro Gulf, the company where he was employed.

Priscilla knew he made a more than substantial salary, and she often wondered why he lived in the beach house, since living there forced him to commute back and forth to Houston every day. He could have afforded something much more modern and closer to his work. But where Priscilla was conventional, Rick Lowrimore was unconventional and did things the way he wanted, not in the way he was expected to do them.

Well, she thought, digging her toes into the wet sand and lifting her face to the breeze, Rick was definitely better off now that he was rid of Angie. Priscilla had known that blonde was a fluffhead from the first moment she'd seen the woman climbing up the stairs to Rick's apartment.

The idea that he was finally rid of her pleased Priscilla immensely, and she smiled at the moon as she rose to her feet. Maybe now she could make Rick see he needed a woman of substance. One with a brain instead of a curvy behind.

* * *

It was well after lunch when Priscilla arrived home from the library. At least fifty preschoolers had shown up to watch the film, and Priscilla was certain all of them had been wiggling, squirming, yelling and giggling at once. Her head was still ringing from the chaos. All she wanted now was to change out of her dress and lie down with a glass of lemonade and a good book.

After changing into a pair of white shorts and a bandeau top, she went to the kitchen to prepare a pitcher of lemonade. Most of her teacher friends were going to take on summer jobs now that school was out, but this summer Priscilla was considering simply doing whatever she got the inclination to do. Her parents had been asking her to come home for a visit for some time now. Maybe she would spend a week or two with them, perhaps see some of her old friends back in Jefferson.

Priscilla had lived in Galveston for three years and had made several good friends through her job at the elementary school. But all considering, she supposed Rick was her very best friend, and had been from the first day he'd moved in. He'd knocked on her door, announced he was going to be her new neighbor, then presented her with a little philodendron vine planted in a ceramic bullfrog. Priscilla had invited him in for coffee, and they'd been fast friends from that moment on.

Priscilla wasn't exactly sure why she and Rick

had hit it off so well. They were not at all alike, and yet that didn't seem to matter. Priscilla could relax and be herself with Rick as she could with no one else. He didn't expect her to be talented or beautiful. And she supposed it was the same for Rick. He'd once told her that she was the only woman who didn't nag him about his cruddy housekeeping and his eating barefooted at the dinner table.

With the lemonade finished, she carried it and the paperback she'd been reading out on the deck. The faded white clapboard house was built on sturdy poles several feet up off the beach, so that it would be safe from the high tides. This afternoon the gulf wind was whipping up the waves and a few white fluffs of clouds could be seen on the far horizon. Sea gulls screeched along the shoreline, swooping down every now and then for a snack of fish.

It was a beautiful view, one that Priscilla never tired of. In fact, she considered herself lucky to live where she did. This particular beach was private, reserved for those who lived along it, so she wasn't bothered by the crowds of tourists that flocked to Galveston each year to play in the sun and the ocean.

The telephone rang just as she settled down on a lounge chair and began to read. With a disgruntled oath, Priscilla tossed the book aside and hurried into the living room.

"Hello."

"Prissy, is that you?"

Priscilla immediately recognized her sister Tracie's voice. "Of course it's me. Who did you expect?"

"You didn't sound like yourself."

"I've just hurried in from outside."

"Well, how are you, sis? We haven't heard from you in a while."

Priscilla supposed that "we" meant the whole family. "I wrote Mom just last week. Is anything wrong?"

"No," Tracie hastened to assure her. "Nothing serious, that is."

Since Priscilla rarely heard from her older sister, she was suddenly on guard. "Tracie, is something going on that I should know about?"

There was a long pause, then Tracie wailed, "I really don't know if you'd care, even if you did know."

Priscilla recognized this side of her sister. She always used that condescending tone whenever she wanted something.

"What does that mean?" Priscilla asked.

Tracie's sniff had a pouty sound to it that had Priscilla rolling her eyes. "Well since you've moved to Galveston, I don't really think you care anything about the family anymore.''

Priscilla had to bite her tongue to keep from reminding her sister that since Tracie had made her home in Dallas, working as an interior decorator, she'd hardly made time for anyone but herself. "Is that why you called, to lecture me?''

"No. No, of course not. I've just missed you. How have you been, sis?''

Priscilla relaxed against the chintz couch. "School is almost out now, so I'm finally going to have some leisure time on my hands. I've been thinking of going home to Jefferson to spend a few days with Mom and Dad.''

"Thank God!'' Tracie exclaimed.

The obvious relief in her sister's voice brought a frown to Priscilla's face. "All right, Tracie, out with it. What's this call really about?''

Sighing, Tracie said, "It's about my sanity, that's what! Mother is on this crazy kick about wanting grandchildren.''

"Hmm,'' Priscilla said, surprised by her sister's disclosure. "This is the first I've heard about it.''

A deprecating snort came across the line. "That's because I'm the one she expects to get married and give her one! She's constantly calling, wanting to know who I'm dating, if I'm serious, if I'm thinking of my biological clock, and—''

Tracie's words were interrupted by Priscilla's

giggles. "Tracie, you're only twenty-eight. Not thirty-eight."

"I've tried telling her that, but she doesn't seem to listen."

"That surprises me," Priscilla said, her laughter fading. "She's never mentioned anything like this to me."

Tracie snorted once again. "That's because she knows there's not any hope of you getting yourself attached to a man!"

"Thanks, Tracie, you always did know how to make me feel good," Priscilla said dryly.

"Oh, you know what I mean, Prissy. You're the brainy sort, and men never interested you that much."

How did Tracie know that? Priscilla wondered irritably. Her sister had never really bothered to ask her how she really felt about anything. She'd always been too busy being prom queen, football queen, class president and the girl most likely to succeed. "Don't you mean I never attracted men like you did?"

"I didn't say that, but now that you've brought it up, have you been dating anyone?"

Priscilla's mind recalled her last outing with the opposite sex. It had been with Williard, the sixth-grade math teacher. He'd kissed her twice and she'd felt about as turned on as a cold fish. "Not anyone on a steady basis."

"Why not?"

Priscilla scooted to the edge of the seat. "What do you mean, why not? Because I don't want to, that's why not. Men are nice, but there are plenty of other things in life just as interesting."

As soon as the words were out she thought of Rick. She didn't know why, but his darkly tanned face with its mocking smile drifted in front of her mind. He'd laugh, and then scold her for saying such a thing.

"God, Prissy, you're still just as stuffy as you ever were! At twenty-five you should be kicking up your heels. Besides," Tracie added, her voice a touch wheedling, "if you had a steady boyfriend maybe mother would get off my back and force her attention on you."

Priscilla's lips pressed together as she stared across the small living room. "So that's what this is all about," she said tightly. She should have known Tracie wasn't calling just to have a sisterly chat.

"And what's wrong if it is? You're the one who loves children. You teach the little monsters every day. Mother should see that you're the maternal one, not me."

It was true that Priscilla did love children, but that didn't mean she wanted to have one just to appease her sister and her mother. "If you ask me, this whole thing is ridiculous. I can't imagine Mom giving you that much of a problem.''

Tracie's laugh was indignant. ''That's what you think! Look, Priscilla, I've taken about all I can stand. When you go home to visit make sure you tell her that you're dating—seriously.''

''But I'm not! And I won't lead her on just to make things easier for you. Besides, it will be at least two weeks before I could leave—''

''Priscilla—honey,'' Tracie began in a gentler voice. ''You live much further away from Mother than I. It would be so easy for you to just stretch the truth a little. It will pacify Mom, and ultimately we'll all be happy.''

Priscilla shook her head. ''And will she be happy when she realizes that I'm no closer to marrying now than I was three years ago?''

''We'll cross that bridge when we come to it,'' Tracie said, then quickly added, ''I've got to go, Priscilla. My other line is ringing. I hope to God it isn't Mother again.''

''Tracie!''

Priscilla cursed under her breath as she heard the phone click dead in her ear. It was just like her sister to leave the conversation dangling.

She put the receiver back on its hook while thoughtfully going over all her sister had said. She suspected Tracie was making a mountain out of a molehill. She couldn't imagine their mother putting that much pressure on Tracie to get married and have children. But, then, her parents were growing older, she reasoned. They'd had their two daughters very late in life, so perhaps they were afraid if Tracie didn't marry soon they wouldn't have many years left to enjoy grandchildren.

Well, Priscilla thought, sighing ruefully, no doubt she'd hear from Tracie again. Probably when she least expected it.

After her sister's call, it was a struggle for Priscilla to get her mind back on the novel she'd left outside on the lounge chair. Every few pages her mind would creep back to Tracie's words. Now that she had time to think about it, she found it all rather dismal. Apparently things hadn't changed since she'd moved to Galveston. Tracie was still her mother's favorite, the one she expected to fulfill her expectations as a daughter.

Priscilla had long ago accepted the fact that she wasn't star quality or glamourous like Tracie, or that her teaching job was ho-hum compared to her sister's exciting job. But it still hurt Priscilla to be reminded of the fact. And if Tracie called back, Priscilla decided, she was going to tell her in no uncertain terms she would have to handle her own problems.

When Rick stopped beside the lounge chair, Priscilla was lying on her stomach, sound asleep.

He regarded the glass of iced tea in his hand with a devilish smile.

The ice and amber liquid splashed against the heated skin of Priscilla's back like a small explosion, making her gasp with shock. Rick laughed wickedly.

"Rick! Damn you!"

Priscilla started to bolt upright only to be reminded she'd unbuttoned her bandeau top while she'd been sunning. Flustered, she snatched the piece of cloth to her breasts and glared threateningly up at him.

"Get that ice off me, you monster!"

Still chuckling, Rick squatted down beside her chair and brushed the ice and tea from the indention in the middle of her back. "Now don't be mad at me, honey," he drawled. "You just looked so hot I thought I'd cool you off."

"Sure, Rick. For a moment I'd forgotten what a sweet man you are."

He reached for the ends of her top and proceeded to button it back together for her. His fingers brushed against her warm skin as he worked and Priscilla felt her senses stir. The feelings surprised her. Rick was just a friend; she'd never thought of him as more.

The buttons in place, he smoothed the fabric against her back, then stood back up. "There you go. See, I am a nice guy, after all."

Priscilla scrambled up from the lounge chair before he had a chance to pull some other pestering trick on her. "Did you bring my root beer home?"

Rick watched her swing her legs over the side of the chair then smooth down her white shorts as she stood. Priscilla was short, her figure soft and curvy. She was completely the opposite of the women he'd dated, who were tall, and model-thin. As he looked at Priscilla, he decided she looked far healthier than the emaciated Angie had.

His thoughts took him by surprise. He'd never really noticed Priscilla in a sexual way before. He didn't know why he had now, unless it was the white shorts and skimpy white top against all that brown skin.

"Er—no. I forgot it," he told her, pulling his eyes off her legs and his mind back to her question.

"Rick, I told you—"

"Priscilla, don't scold me! I bought a T-bone steak for you as well as me—they're already on the charcoal."

Sniffing the air, she glanced across to the other side of the deck where the charcoal grill they shared was located. "You bought a steak for me, after I've fed you the last five times we've shared supper? Rick, your thoughtfulness overwhelms me."

He swatted her on the bottom, propelling her in the direction of the door. "Go wash. It's almost ready, and you know how put out I get when you dawdle in the bathroom.''

As Priscilla entered the house she called sassily back at him, ''Rick Lowrimore, you've never had to wait on me in your life.''

Chapter Two

The two of them ate outside on a little round table Rick had found at a flea market in Houston. Priscilla had contributed a pair of webbed lawn chairs she'd discovered on sale in a local discount store. The table and chairs, along with the charcoal grill, were considered mutual property and sat in the middle of their adjoining sun deck.

"Mmm, I'm starved," Rick said as he sliced into his steak. "I didn't have time for lunch today."

"Pushing too many buttons?" she asked. Rick had boiled several ears of corn. Priscilla proceeded to fork one onto her plate and slather it with butter.

"A diesel deal," he answered, chewing with relish. "How did the film go? Did the little ones like it?"

Priscilla's groan was accompanied with a smile. "We had at least fifty crammed into one small room. But it was a big success once we got them quieted down and the movie began to roll."

"I doubt they could have been any louder than a boardroom full of businessmen. How's your steak?"

"Perfect. You're such a good cook, Rick." And it was perfect. Medium-rare, just as she liked.

"You don't have to be patronizing," he said, raking back the blond hair that had fallen across his forehead.

Priscilla glanced up at him in surprise. "I wasn't. It really is perfect. Did I sound dry? I didn't mean to. I guess my mind is wandering."

Rick leaned back against his chair, a glass of tea in his hand. The crushed ice tinkled against the glass as he lifted it to his mouth. "Problem?" he asked after a long drink.

Priscilla shrugged. "I had a call from my sister today."

One of his brows lifted curiously. "You hardly ever mention your sister. Trouble back home?"

Priscilla shook her head. "Not really. It seems my parents are hankering for grandchildren and Mother has been badgering Tracie about it."

"But not you?" he asked, slicing off another bite of steak.

A pink flush spread across Priscilla's tanned

face. "Apparently Mother believes I'm a losing cause in that department. You see, Tracie was always the one with the beauty. She's always attracted men."

Rick's eyes traveled intently over Priscilla. She was usually cheerful and full of spirit. It surprised him to see a gloomy expression cross her face. "Then let her worry about your mother."

Priscilla made a disgruntled sound as she stabbed her fork into the baked potato on her plate. "Tracie is far from the marrying kind. And as for children, she can barely tolerate them." Drawing in a long breath, she looked back at Rick. "She wants me to tell Mother I'm serious about a man, so she'll shift her interest to me. Isn't that laughable?"

"It sounds as if your sister wants you to handle her problems, instead of handling them herself."

"You're right. I should forget the whole thing. And I will."

Rick continued to study her as they ate. The ocean breeze was blowing her bobbed hair in disarray. It was a warm brown color just a shade darker than her gold-brown eyes. She had soft, feminine features. A full mouth that curved slightly up at the corners, her nose was straight and perky, the bridge of it dusted faintly with freckles. At the moment there was a scowl denting the smooth skin between her brows, telling him this thing with her sister had upset her.

Reaching across the table he touched the puckered skin on her forehead. "You're going to get wrinkles. Besides, I'm the one who should be upset. I'm the one who broke up with my girlfriend."

It was obvious he wasn't the least bit upset. Priscilla looked at him pointedly. "I'm glad you brought that up, Rick. I've been wanting to have a talk with you about your women."

Grinning, he nonchalantly reached for the steak sauce. "Oh? Worried about my heart, are you?"

"Rick, I'm serious, so listen to me. It could be more than your ego hurting, if you get hooked to the wrong woman."

"But, Priscilla, sugar, I don't intend getting hooked to any woman—not permanently."

"Even so, just a semipermanent relationship could be dangerous. What if you accidently, and I underscore accidently, fall in love? And then she decides to drop you? It would scar you for life."

Rick clucked his tongue. "Priscilla, you're really worrying unnecessarily. I know what I'm doing."

She gave him a droll look. "Oh? I suppose that's why you're sitting here with me instead of Angie?"

He'd never thought about it that way before. But in all honesty Rick knew he'd rather be sitting here with Priscilla than with Angie. With Priscilla he could be himself. He didn't have to try to impress her the way he did his so-called girlfriends. But, hell, Priscilla knew him like a book anyway. Trying to impress her would never work.

"I wouldn't want to be with Angie if she walked up here right now," he insisted. "She's out of my life for good."

Priscilla sighed with disgust and reached for her glass. "You kept insisting you were crazy about the woman."

He waved away her words as he continued to savor every bite of his steak and potato. "That was only temporary insanity. Nothing more."

"See! Just think how it would be it if you didn't get your sanity back until it was too late."

"Priscilla, are you trying to tell me to stay away from women? You know that's impossible for a man like me."

Her brown eyes glided over the red T-shirt molded to his broad shoulders, his blond hair teased by the breeze and his twinkling blue eyes. The first time she'd seen him, he'd been walking around the place with their landlord, and she thought she'd never seen such a breathtaking man. But now when she looked at Rick she saw much more than his classical good looks. She saw the boyish mischief in his smile when he was teasing her, and the kindness and compassion he showed her when she was worrying over a problem.

There'd even been times when she'd seen him in grief. Especially the time his mother had suddenly passed away from a stroke. It had hurt Priscilla deeply to see him in such pain, and she'd tried her best to keep his mind occupied until enough time had passed to lessen the loss of his mother.

Yes, she thought, Rick was a man who looked like a woman's dream, but she didn't see that anymore. When she looked at Rick she saw the man underneath, the man who was her dearest friend.

"Rick, dear, I only want you to have the right woman, that's all."

He gave her a dreary look. "Priscilla, I don't see you making straight *A*'s in the love department. How long has it been since you've even dated?"

She bristled. "For your information, I went with Williard to the movies six weeks ago."

"Williard," he drawled mockingly. "I could blow him over with one breath."

"I didn't go out with him for his muscles, Rick!"

He forked the last bite of steak to his mouth. "I don't know why you went out with him period."

"Well, maybe I can't attract droves of men," she blurted out, a bit hurt, even though she knew it was ridiculous to be. "But I do know about women, because I am one. And you've been barking up the wrong tree!'' Flustered, she tossed down the ear of corn and scraped back her chair. ''If you're finished, let's get this mess cleaned up,'' she said sharply.

Rick could see that she was really put out with him, but he wasn't sure why. He'd always been able to say whatever he wanted to Priscilla without worrying about offending her. This time shouldn't have been any different.

''I bought a cake at the deli,'' he said, after a moment of tense silence. ''Let's have a piece before we do the dishes.''

Priscilla almost refused, but a grin suddenly dimpled his face, and she wasn't the type to pout even if her feelings had been pricked. ''What kind is it?''

Chuckling, he got to his feet. ''Devil's food with cream-cheese icing.''

''I'll make coffee,'' she said. Rising from her chair, she began to collect their dirty plates.

Rick helped her and in moments they were carrying it all into his kitchen. While Priscilla filled a glass carafe with cold water, Rick spooned ground coffee into the coffeemaker.

Priscilla was as accustomed to his kitchen as she was to hers, and they worked side by side, easily and efficiently. Once the coffee was dripping and filling the room with a rich aroma, Rick brought out the cake. Priscilla sliced into it and placed two hefty pieces on dessert plates.

"Priscilla, I'm sorry I made fun of Williard," he said as they carried their cake and coffee back out to the table on the sun deck. "I just happen to think you deserve better than him."

It was impossible to remain indifferent to Rick, even for a few minutes. Priscilla looked across at him and smiled as they took their seats. "I happen to think that you do, too, Rick. I want you to have a woman who will really care for you, not just care about what you might give her."

Laughter gurgled in Rick's throat as he dug into his cake. "Pris, I'm not ready for a wife, and it sounds like that's what you're trying to find for me."

"Not at all. I just want you to have—the right companion."

He smiled, and Priscilla didn't miss the gleam in his eyes. "Maybe we should make a deal," Rick suggested. "You pick out my next girlfriend and I'll pick you a man."

Priscilla's mouth fell open and her eyes grew wide. "A—a man!" she spluttered. "Rick, you're crazy. I don't want a man."

"How do you know? You've never had one worth wanting."

"Rick!" she scolded, her lips pressed in a rigid line. "Sometimes you can be so coarse!"

"Well," he said with a shrug and a roguish smile. "You know it's true."

She continued to scowl at him. Rick forked off a piece of his cake and lifted it over to her mouth. After a moment of his coaxing, she gave in and let him feed it to her.

"What do you say?" he asked. "It might be fun to see how well we could pick partners for each other."

Priscilla grabbed his coffee cup and sniffed. "Have you put something alcoholic in this? I think you're drunk."

Laughter rolled from Rick. "Pris, you're the most amusing woman I know."

Not sexy. Not beautiful. But amusing, she thought with resignation. "That's because I'm the only woman friend you have."

He chewed the cake with sinful enjoyment as his eyes twinkled back at her. "Nonsense. What do you call Angie and all the others?"

"Statistics."

Rick tried to look offended, but there was laughter in his blue eyes. "Be serious," he scolded.

"Okay, they were only sex objects."

He had to admit she was right. And that left him with nothing to say. Besides, it amazed him that Priscilla was so damn smart where he was concerned. She seemed to always know things about him that he'd never noticed or cared to notice about himself. "Is that what Williard was? Your sex object?"

The question was so ridiculous that Priscilla nearly choked on her cake. "Williard? He's probably a virgin."

She probably was too, Rick thought, and for some reason found himself smiling at the idea. After the list of experienced women he'd known in the past, it was refreshing to know that Priscilla was chaste, her standards high.

"You could probably change that," he mused.

Priscilla's face wrinkled with distaste. "For Williard? I hardly think so! He's a sweet man, but I don't intend to spend the rest of my life with a man who eats the same cereal for breakfast three hundred and sixty-five days a year, and spends every Saturday afternoon cleaning out his parakeet cage."

Chuckling, Rick leaned back in his chair, both hands cradled around his coffee cup. "You see, you really should let me pick someone out for you."

Priscilla downed her last bite of cake and pushed away her plate. "Blind dates are out of style. Besides, I know you, Rick. You'd pick out some wolf I'd have to fight off all night long."

"Sex is nice, Priscilla. Contrary to your beliefs. Besides, if we turned the coin you'd have me dating someone who thought an exciting evening was holding hands and reading Yeats.''

She tried to keep her expression mocking, but it was difficult to do. The image of Rick reading Yeats to a woman was ridiculously funny. ''Would it hurt you to spend one evening that way?''

One dark blond brow arched at Priscilla. ''Hurt me? It would put me to sleep. Would it hurt you to spend one night with a wolf?''

She shot him a demeaning glare. ''Just give me advance notice so I can be working out with my weights.'' She flexed her bicep at him. ''He'd never know what hit him.''

Rick smiled, but there was no amusement in his eyes as they traveled along her shoulders and arms, the curvy outline of her full breast. She was toasty brown, her skin satiny smooth. He could very well imagine a man wanting to touch her. Funny that he suddenly found the idea so distasteful. If he did pick a date for her, he'd be sure and tell the man to keep his hands in his pockets. Priscilla was above all that, and he'd waylay any man who tried to take advantage of her.

''Don't worry, Priscilla. I'd never pick a wolf for you.'' Rising from his chair, he reached over and grabbed her hand. ''But for now let's walk down by the seawall and watch the tourists come and go.''

She allowed him to pull her to her feet and down

the stairs. "We haven't finished the dishes. And don't you have business papers to go over?" she asked.

"Dear Priscilla, while you're in bed at ten o'clock tonight, I'll slave over my work."

Starting across the beach, they headed west toward the main part of town. As they walked, Rick tucked Priscilla's hand in the crook of his arm. She looked up at him, her eyes glinting impishly.

"You need to get more rest, Rick. You're going to get old before your time."

With a low laugh, he covered her hand with his and gave it a little reproving squeeze. "And you need to have more fun, Pris. Or you're going to wrinkle up like an old prune."

She continued to smile up at him. "Some people like the taste of prunes. Just remember that, Rick, when you're picking me out a date."

Two days later Priscilla was carrying in her groceries when the telephone rang. She answered it, half expecting it to be her friend Lori, only to find it was her mother.

"Mom! How nice to hear from you. Are you and Dad doing okay? Did you get my letter?"

"Yes, dear, we're both fine. You're so sweet to write so regularly. However, I've been expecting you to call and say you're coming up for a visit."

Priscilla edged the sack in her arms onto the

corner of the table, then shifted the phone to a more comfortable position against her ear. "I'm planning on it, Mom. As soon as school is out."

"When will that be?"

"This week is the last."

"That's perfect. I was thinking about coming down there for a few days. That is, if I wouldn't be imposing? It's been so long since I've gotten to spend any time with you. And it's so pleasant there on the beach."

Priscilla's mind began churning. This wasn't like her mother, at all. She never left her husband's side for anything—not even her daughters.

"That—that would be nice, Mom. But what about Dad?"

"Well, you know that ordinarily I wouldn't leave your father, but he's going on a fishing trip with your Uncle Hershall. He won't miss me at all," she said quickly.

"Well," Priscilla began slowly, "that sounds great."

"I thought so too, honey. And isn't it wonderful that the opportunity for me to come for a visit has happened at such a perfect time."

Priscilla began taking the groceries out of the paper sack. She'd purchased fresh spinach for a salad, eggplant to fry in a beer batter and a package of chicken breasts. Two for Rick and one for her. "Why do you say that?"

Her mother's laughter tinkled slyly. "Don't try to play innocent, Pris. Tracie's already let the cat out of the bag."

Priscilla went stock-still. "What are you talking about?"

"Now, Pris, there's no need to keep it a secret. You should have known how pleased your father and I would be."

Priscilla groped for a chair, then sank down onto the edge of it. "Pleased? About what?"

Gloria Parker's laughter trilled again. "Your engagement, Pris! How could you keep something like that a secret for so long? Especially knowing how thrilled it would make me?"

Priscilla was suddenly coughing. How could Tracie do this to her? she silently seethed. She was going to kill her sister! Absolutely kill her! With grim determination she swallowed, mentally preparing herself to tell her mother the truth. Yet before she could utter a word, her mother spoke again.

"You can't imagine how shocked I was when Tracie called to give me the news. I never suspected you'd been seeing anyone, and I'd given up hope on—"

Her mother's voice broke off abruptly. Priscilla had opened her mouth to speak, when Gloria began again. This time there were tears in her voice. "Well, darling Pris, I'm just so happy and proud of you. Someone to love you and a family of your own. It's what I've always wished for you, sweetheart. And I can't begin to tell you how much I'll enjoy having a grandchild.''

Priscilla's soft heart felt as if it were torn down the middle. What was she going to do? She hated to come right out and burst her mother's bubble of happiness, she thought desperately. And if she told her that Tracie had deliberately lied to her, she'd be even more hurt.

She was trying to think of something to say, when Gloria's voice came back in her ear. This time excitement was added to her tears. ''I can't wait to meet him! What's he like?''

As much as Priscilla wanted to, she couldn't bring herself to disappoint her mother with the truth. ''Uh, well, he's very good-looking. Very smart. I'm sure you'll love him as much as I do.''

''Well, what does he do? How old is he?''

Priscilla nervously licked her lips. ''I—I want to keep that a secret until you get here. I want to surprise you. But right now I've got to go. He's coming for supper and I haven't started cooking yet.''

''That's my girl. Feed him up good. You'll keep him contented that way,'' Gloria said happily.

Priscilla had to stifle a groan. ''Er—when should I look for you, Mother?''

"If everything goes as planned, Friday evening."

Four days away. What was she going to do? "I'll look forward to seeing you, Mother. Tell Dad hello and give him my love."

"Of course I will, darling. And he's very happy about your engagement. He's already set to give you a big wedding. Flowers, champagne—everything our little girl deserves."

Priscilla passed a weary hand over her face. "I—we'll talk all about it when you get here," she said, trying to keep her voice light and convincing.

"I can't wait, Priscilla. See you Friday."

"Bye, Mother. Love you." Priscilla hung the phone up without waiting to hear the click at the other end.

Damn Tracie! Didn't she have any idea what this was going to do to their parents?

For a few moments Priscilla simply sat there holding her head in her hands, her mind spinning. Her mother was coming to Galveston, expecting to find her with a fiancé. The whole idea was insane. She couldn't even come up with a boyfriend, much less a fiancé. She had to do something, and fast!

Quickly she put the groceries away, then dialed her sister's number. The answering machine cut in on the third ring, and she heard Tracie's cheery voice informing anyone who happened to call that she'd be out for the evening. Priscilla slammed down the phone and began to pace throughout the house.

Glancing at her watch, she noticed it was nearly seven o'clock. Normally she would have dinner almost prepared. Rick would be coming home soon and Rick! He would know what to do, she thought with relief.

Priscilla hurried outside and down the steps to wait for him.

Rick drummed his fingers restlessly against the steering wheel and hummed along with a popular rock tune playing on the car radio. Just a few more miles and he'd be home.

His mind drifted longingly to a tall, cool drink and ridding himself of his shirt and tie. Priscilla would have their supper ready, he thought contentedly. It would probably be meatballs and pasta, because she hadn't fixed that in a while and it was one of his favorites.

He glanced down on the seat beside him at the two six-packs of diet root beer. She was going to be in a state of shock when he gave them to her. The idea brought a faint grin to his mouth.

Rick loved to shock Priscilla, mainly because he knew how much she enjoyed acting indignant with him. He often called her stuffy, but in actuality he was only teasing. Priscilla wasn't stuffy, at all. In fact, she had a very open mind about nearly everything. It was one of the first nice things he'd discovered about Priscilla. The only thing he could think of that she didn't have an open mind about was men. And he couldn't understand that. Priscilla was a lovely girl, but she chose to shut herself away from the male race.

Today Rick had casually mentioned to his working cronies that he had a pretty single neighbor. But none of them had been interested in going out on a date with her. They'd all seemed to think if she was as good as Rick made her sound, he would have already had her for himself.

Their attitude had made him see this picking a partner thing was going to be much more difficult than he had first imagined.

Priscilla was sitting on the bottom step of his staircase when he drove up. She immediately stood up and ran toward the car as he parked it under the shelter of the sun deck. The ocean breeze swirled her yellow sundress around her calves and molded it to her shapely thighs.

As Rick cut the motor, his gaze traveled appreciatively down the length of her, then back up to her face. It was his buddies' loss, Rick thought. Priscilla was a lovely girl.

Chapter Three

"Rick! Thank God you're home," she said in a rush.

He lifted out his briefcase stuffed with papers, tossed his blazer over his shoulder, then locked the door behind him. "Hello, Pris," he said easily, turning and bestowing a casual kiss on her cheek. "Is something wrong?"

"Oh, yes! Yes! You can't possibly imagine." She grabbed for his arm and clutched it tightly. "You've got to help me find a way out of this mess, Rick. I'm desperate, I tell you."

His fingers reached up and worked at his tie as, together they climbed the steps. "Sugar, you sound more stirred up than that time you thought you were going to have to teach sex education to a class of teenagers."

"Rick! This isn't a time to joke!"

He patted the soft hand clutching his arm. "Don't worry, Pris. You can tell me all about it and I'm sure we'll be able to come up with some perfectly simple solution."

They reached the front door to Rick's duplex and Priscilla followed him inside. Even in her frantic state of mind she could still appreciate how handsome he looked in his light gray trousers, white shirt and dark gray suspenders. The wind had blown his wavy hair down over one eye, but he ignored the pestering lock as he tugged off his tie and tossed it toward the couch.

Where Priscilla's apartment was neat and organized, Rick's was a maze of strewn papers, books, dirty glasses and clothes, not to mention records, cassette tapes, a set of barbells and a compound bow. Only Lord knew where he could use a compound bow in Galveston.

"Do you have supper ready?" he asked as he headed out of the living room and toward the bath.

"No," Priscilla called after him. "I was too upset to cook."

"Priscilla," he groaned with disappointment. "I just knew you'd make meatballs and pasta. Am I going to have to get on my knees and beg?"

"Rick, you sound like a complaining husband. We'll eat later. Now hurry and come out of there."

"Do you want to give me time to put on some clothes, or shall I come out naked?"

Priscilla nearly tripped over the barbells as she tried to make her way to the couch. "I can only take one shock a day, Rick. Go ahead and dress," she said loud enough for him to hear.

She sat down on the couch to wait, trying her best to keep from wringing her hands in nervous agitation.

"Okay, Pris. What's this all about?" he asked, coming back into the room.

He'd changed into a pair of white gym shorts and a ragged orange University of Texas sweatshirt with the arms cut out. Taking a seat next to Priscilla, he began to pull a pair of tennis shoes onto his bare feet.

"I've got to find a fiancé. Fast," Priscilla blurted out.

Rick raised his head slowly, a blank look on his face. "What? Did you say fiancé?"

Priscilla nodded grimly. "I'm afraid so."

He finished tying his shoelaces, then straightened back up. The urge to burst out laughing was quickly smothered by the stricken look on her face. "Sugar, are you serious? Why would you need a fiancé unless you—" Disbelief widened his eyes. "Priscilla, my God, I thought you were a virgin!"

"Damn it, Rick, don't be crazy! The last thing I am is pregnant."

He looked visibly relieved. "Then—" he reached up and raked back his wayward hair "—I think you'd better tell me the whole thing from the beginning."

Priscilla scooted to the edge of the couch while Rick leaned back against the cushions. "It's Tracie. She called our mother and told her I was engaged to be married. Now Mother is coming here to Galveston to meet him. Oh, Rick," she moaned miserably, "what am I going to do?"

He made an exasperated face. "What any normal person would do, Pris. You're going to get on the phone, call your mother and tell her just how things really are."

Priscilla's head jerked back and forth. "I can't, Rick. I just can't."

Seeing the agony in her eyes, Rick leaned up and took her by the shoulders. "You can. Go to the phone and do it. That would be much better than waiting until she gets here to hit her with the truth."

Unable to accept his suggestion, Priscilla jumped to her feet. "You don't understand, Rick. She—she was so happy and excited she was actually in tears. She kept asking about him—the fiancé—and—" She looked at the ceiling and drew in a ragged breath. "She says Daddy wants me to have champagne and flowers." She looked back at Rick and suddenly there were tears in her eyes.

"Can you imagine, Rick? My parents are actually proud of me, for probably the very first time in my life."

Rick couldn't stand seeing Priscilla like this. She was usually so happy and never unflappable. She was the sensible one, while he was the one who strayed off track. He didn't know how to handle this reversal in their characters.

Rising to his feet, he put his arms around her. "Pris, you're talking crazy. Of course your parents are proud of you," he said gently. "You don't need a man for that."

Priscilla sniffed and smiled shakily at him. "You don't know, Rick. I've never been like Tracie, never had her accomplishments—"

"Priscilla, you aren't engaged to anyone, and frankly I think your sister is a rat for doing such a thing. Your parents need to know just exactly what a dirty trick she's pulled."

Priscilla's shaky smile faded completely. "Tracie is their princess. It would hurt them even more, to know she's not the perfect daughter they think she is."

"Priscilla," he began, reaching up and tucking the stray lock of hair on her cheek back behind her ear, "I know you want to make your parents happy, but—"

She turned in his arms, looking up at his handsome face. "Rick, you're my dearest friend. You have to help me out of this. I've got to find some-one—anyone—who'd be willing to act as my fi-ancé. It would just be for a few days, while my mother is here.''

Rick frowned at her. ''And what's going to hap-pen later—when it comes time for a wedding?''

''I'll worry about that later. I can always say we broke up.''

''And that won't disappoint them?'' he asked, amazed at her reasoning.

''Maybe—a little. But maybe by then I will have a real fiancé,'' she said bravely.

Rick wanted to shake her. Instead he looked at her through narrowed eyes. ''What do you mean by that? You plan to grab the first man who comes along, just to please your parents?''

Pulling away from him, she began to pace around the cluttered room. ''Well, Williard wants to marry me,'' she said, more to herself than to Rick.

Rick stared after her. ''Williard! My God, Pris-cilla, you've gone mad. You were just telling me what a bore he was.''

She turned and glared at him. ''I didn't say I was going to marry Williard. I only said he wanted to marry me. At least I know there's one out there.''

Rick would kill scrawny Williard before he'd let his Priscilla marry a man like that. ''Forget about the real thing,'' he told her gruffly. ''Would Williard be willing to act—for a few days?''

Priscilla thought about it for a few moments, then shook her head. ''I wouldn't even ask. He's very straitlaced and wouldn't dream of committing any kind of deception—even a well-meaning one. Besides, he would want to make the whole thing real.''

''We're crossing Williard off,'' Rick said firmly. ''What other men do you know who might be willing to pose as your fiancé.''

Priscilla threw up her hands helplessly. ''I've been thinking for hours. Of course I know several men teachers, but—but I can't imagine any of them acting as my fiancé. Most of them are already married. There is one that's getting a divorce, but he's—unacceptable. What about your friends, Rick? Is there anyone you can think of that might be willing to help me out?''

He hadn't even been able to get one to agree to go out on a date with Priscilla, much less parade in front of her mother as her intended. But he could hardly tell her that. He could already see how fragile her ego was in that department. ''Not really,'' he mumbled, then his face brightened as another idea came to him. ''You could hire an actor. That way no friends or unwanted feelings would be involved.''

Priscilla stopped her pacing to look at him.

"That sounds well and good, Rick. But even if I could find an actor who'd be willing to play the part, I couldn't afford him. Certainly not for a week's work."

"A week!" Rick echoed. "You mean this—man will have to hang around for a week?"

Priscilla shrugged helplessly. "Off and on. I mean, it only stands to reason that a mother would want to see her future son-in-law as much as possible while she's here."

"I see what you mean," he reluctantly agreed. "But things would be much simpler if it was only for a one-time meeting—maybe for dinner. We might be able to come up with someone just for one evening, but—"

Priscilla shook her head in frustration. "If it was you in this mess, it wouldn't be a problem at all. You'd just open that black book of yours and pick out a name. But with me, it's hopeless."

Sighing, Rick crossed the room and took Priscilla by the arm. "Let's get out of here. I'm starving and I can't think when I'm starving. Why don't we walk down and have a hamburger? We can come up with something while we eat."

Priscilla passed a hand over her forehead. "I'm sorry about supper, Rick. I'd planned to have a lovely meal with spinach salad and—"

"Forget it," he said, squeezing her shoulder.

"I'll do the cooking tonight. Fries, shakes and hamburgers with lots of onions."

Smiling ruefully she followed him out the door. "You're so sweet, Rick."

"I know, sugar, that's what all the women tell me," he teased, hoping to lighten her mood.

Priscilla tried to laugh, but the only thing that came out was a groan. She kept imagining the devastated look on her mother's face when she had to tell her that one of her daughters was a liar and the other a failure with men.

Minutes later they were sitting in a small restaurant on Seawall Boulevard. Their booth overlooked the ocean, and Priscilla watched the white-crested waves roll in on the beach as the sun disappeared in the west.

"I've never seen you looking so glum, Priscilla, and frankly I hate it."

She looked at him while absently fidgeting with her water glass. "I don't like being glum," she admitted.

"Then don't be."

Sighing, she leaned back against the vinyl cushion of the booth. "Rick, you just don't understand. I know this whole thing probably seems very trivial to you, but to me—"

Rick made a tsk-ing noise as he studied the misery on Priscilla's features. "What puzzles me the most about this whole thing is that you can't go to your mother and be totally honest with her. I could always tell my parents anything.''

Priscilla opened her mouth to reply just as the waitress arrived with their food. When the woman walked away, Rick reached for the pepper shaker while cocking an eye back to Priscilla. ''You were going to say?''

''Just that my childhood was probably very different from yours. You didn't have a sister.''

He plopped the bun back on his hamburger, then after second thought opened it back up and squeezed ketchup over the lot. ''I didn't have a brother, either. So?''

''Much to my parents' horror, I was a tomboy up until about thirteen years old,'' she said.

''Then hormones invaded and changed all that.''

''Well, to some degree,'' she admitted in a dejected voice. ''I started to develop into a young woman but—but I didn't blossom into a beautiful swan like Tracie. That's when the problems really started. My parents wanted me to follow in her footsteps. I couldn't, and furthermore I didn't want to, but they couldn't see that. At least not for a while. Tracie could sing, play the clarinet, dance—''

''What did you do?'' he asked, frowning. He didn't like hearing Priscilla put herself down.

She picked up her hamburger and forced herself

to take a bite. Eating was the last thing on her mind, but she knew Rick would have a fit if she didn't make an effort toward the food on her plate. "Well, I liked to fish and I was good at that, but Mom said fishing was a man's interest and that I should turn my attention to more feminine things. So Daddy quit letting me go on fishing trips with him. Then there was softball. I was good at that and even made the main string at school, but Mom said that was far too rough a sport for her daughter to compete in."

Rick gave a grunt of disbelief. "That's ridiculous. Softball is a wonderful sport. It's an American pastime."

Priscilla nodded. "I know," she said wryly. "But you see, when I was in high school my parents were already in their fifties. My mother's ideas were, and still are, a bit stodgy. And you have to remember that Tracie was taking jazz and tap dancing, was a soprano in the glee club and received top honors in band. My parents wanted me to develop a talent also. But the only real talent I had was in history and geography class."

Rick regarded her closely as he swirled a French fry around in a pool of ketchup. "No one can be someone else. You should never have tried. And there's nothing wrong with being a history brain. By being a teacher, you've put it to good use."

Priscilla rubbed her fingers tiredly across her

eyes. "Yes, I know, but I wanted desperately to make my parents as proud of me as they were of Tracie."

"But that didn't mean you needed to be like her. They should have let you do your own thing in your own way."

With a heavy sigh, Priscilla looked across at him. "That's probably true. But I let them down so many times in the past that I just can't let them down this time."

Rick shook his head wearily back and forth. "Priscilla, this is screwball, and so unlike you. What are you going to do? Marry some man you don't love, just to please your parents?"

She wrinkled her nose at him. "No. Right now I'll just do a bit of pretending. Then, later, I'm going to make a concentrated effort to find the right man for me. If you remember, it was only last night that you were telling me that I should date more."

Rick wasn't liking the tone of this at all. "I said dating. That's a hell of a lot different than walking down the aisle."

She drew her shoulders up with determination. "You also said I should try sex. You said it was nice. And you know me, Rick, I could never enter into a sexual relationship unless I was married to the man."

Rick grabbed his milkshake, nearly sloshing it

onto the table. "Priscilla, that was only twenty-four hours ago that we were having that discussion. You weren't at all interested then, now suddenly you are. You've let this whole thing muddle your thinking."

"Oh, it's muddled me all right," she said tersely. "Maybe it's also shaken my eyes open. But that's beside the point. Right now I need a man. Desperately!"

Rick's glance darted wildly around the small restaurant, wondering if any of the diners had overheard her remark. Good Lord, they probably thought she was a nymphomaniac. "Shh, Pris! Do you want the men in here to hear you? The cops will probably be down here in a few minutes to pick you up for soliciting!"

Unaffected by his warnings, Priscilla's face suddenly brightened. "That's it, Rick! I'll advertise for a fiancé. Maybe I can get an ad in the paper before it goes to press tonight. Should I try the *Houston Chronicle?* Which one do you think would be best?"

"No! I absolutely forbid it!" Rick nearly shouted. "You're not that kind of girl, Priscilla."

This time Priscilla glanced around the room to see several pairs of eyes had turned their way. "Rick," she began patiently and under her breath. "I won't be advertising for a sexual liaison."

"But that is exactly what every man that reads

it will think. I won't let you do such a stupid thing."

She was suddenly angry with him. He wasn't helping her at all. He was only narrowing down the choices, making her feel even more desperate. "And who are you to tell me what I can or cannot do, Rick Lowrimore?" she asked icily.

He set his milkshake back down with a plunk and stared her in the eye. "Your new fiancé."

Shock caused Priscilla's jaw to drop, her brown eyes to widen. "My—my what?" she repeated blankly.

"You heard me, Priscilla. I don't know why I didn't think of this before. We've been racking our brains over this, when all the time I was the perfect solution," he said smugly, the look on his face reflecting how proud he was of himself for solving her problem.

"But—you're my neighbor. My friend. You can't be my fiancé!"

Rick's expression was suddenly exasperated. "And why not? Who could be a better choice? Just think about it, Priscilla. I know all about your family, their names, where you grew up and so forth. I know all your nasty little habits, your likes and dislikes. Why, I know more about you than most real fiancés know about the women they marry. It will be a snap to play the part of your loving betrothed."

Priscilla's mind was suddenly whirling. What would her mother think when she arrived and found Rick by her side? She'd never believe it! "I'm sorry, Rick, but it would never work," she said dismally.

"But why ever not? I'm a man. I'll be easily accessible all week."

"Rick, my mother would take one look at you and know that I could have never found a man like you to love me."

A scowl settled across his features. "You're getting pathetic on me now, and I don't like it. Of course a man like me could love a woman like you."

Priscilla pushed away the remains of her food. That was so easy for him to say, she thought. But reality was far different. Rick was a smart man, he should know that. "Rick, I'm chopped liver. You're a man who can, and is accustomed to, having New York strips."

"I didn't know we were discussing a side of beef," he said, his voice sarcastic.

"Come on, Rick, you know what I mean. You've never dated a woman who looked like me. And I've never gone out with a man who looked like you."

"There's nothing wrong with the way you look. But what's wrong with me?" he wanted to know, glancing down at himself with mild surprise.

"You—you look like a playboy," Priscilla said, suddenly averting her eyes from his blue ones. To think of Rick as her love interest was—more than disturbing. "And playboys aren't attracted to plain women."

"Priscilla, that's a very degrading remark about both of us," he said, then grinned in afterthought. "Maybe I should go down tomorrow and purchase a pair of eyeglasses."

Reaching over, he pulled a few fries from Priscilla's plate and plopped them in his mouth. Priscilla concluded from his relaxed attitude that he apparently considered the whole problem taken care of.

"And maybe I should go purchase a few glamourous clothes or a new hairdo," she said mockingly.

Her words sparked a thought in his mind. "What about a ring, Pris? That's probably the first thing she'll want to see."

Priscilla had been so worried about finding a man, she hadn't even thought about an engagement ring. "Oh, I'll go downtown and get one of those cubic zirconia stones. She'll never know the difference."

"Don't get anything tacky," he insisted. "I don't want her thinking I have bad taste."

Amazed, she stared at him. "This is pretend, Rick," she reminded.

"I know. But to your mother it will be real."

"Maybe you should pick it out," she suggested dryly.

He nodded. "You're right, I will. I'll go downtown tomorrow on my lunch break."

He was serious! Priscilla's head was virtually swimming. She'd been so worried about all this and now to have Rick as her fiancé, even in pretense, was mind-boggling.

"Pris, did you hear? Is that all right with you?"

She jerked her mind back on his words. "Er— yes, I guess so. I'll give you a signed check."

"Don't worry about it," he said. "I'll keep the receipt and you can pay me later."

He suddenly smiled and Priscilla shook her head. "I don't like that silly grin on your face, Rick. This is not an amusing matter."

A hurt look, obviously feigned, took the smile off his mouth. "I don't think it's amusing. I'm smiling because I think it's going to be fun."

"Fun! You've spent the past two hours trying to tell me the whole idea was crazy!"

But that was before he was going to be the fiancé, Rick reasoned with himself. That changed matters completely. Now he wouldn't have to worry about Priscilla getting herself into something with another man. Especially something she wouldn't know how to handle.

"I still think your plan is crazy. I'm just no

longer worried, now that I know I'll be around to watch over you.''

Priscilla wasn't quite sure why Rick thought he needed to watch over her, but at the moment she was too tired to ask. Hiding a yawn behind her hand, she said, ''Let's go home, Rick. I want to go to bed.''

''At this hour! Priscilla—''

Suddenly the waitress appeared at the side of the table with their check, making Rick break off as he glanced up at the woman.

''We've just become engaged,'' he told the middle-aged woman. ''Care to congratulate us?''

''Rick!'' Priscilla gasped. What in the world was he doing, she wondered frantically.

The waitress glanced from Rick to Priscilla's gaping face, then back to Rick. ''Congratulations,'' she said with a wink. ''I hope you have many happy years together.''

''Thank you,'' he said, his face beaming.

Talk about an actor, Priscilla groaned inwardly. Rick was already giving an award performance.

The waitress moved away and Rick picked up the check. ''Shall we go, Pris?'' he asked blithely, while rising to his feet.

Without a word, Priscilla followed. They paused at the register long enough for Rick to pay for their meal, then stepped out into the warm night air.

''Rick!'' she burst out, finally finding her voice

as they stepped onto the asphalt parking lot of the restaurant. "Tomorrow I'm making a doctor's appointment for you. Clearly you need psychiatric help!"

Laughing, he grabbed her hand and swung it playfully back and forth between them. "I was practicing, Priscilla. There's no harm in practicing."

After glancing both ways for oncoming traffic, he tugged her across the wide street so that they could walk along the sidewalk built upon the high seawall.

"There is harm!" Priscilla insisted. "We go into that particular restaurant together quite often."

"So they'll think we're engaged. What does that hurt?"

"But we aren't and—"

"Look, Priscilla, you started this game of pretense. You might as well get used to it."

Priscilla stared dismally at the sidewalk as they walked back toward home. "Yes, I know, but I thought the pretense would be contained to only my mother."

He shook his head. "I'm afraid it can't be."

She glanced up at him as they skirted around a group of people on the sidewalk. "What do you mean?"

"Think about it. If your mother intends to stay a week, it's a surefire bet she's going to see or talk to some of your friends. Maybe even some of mine. Who knows who might pop up for a visit. We're going to have to tell people we're engaged. For real. Or she's bound to pick up on something.''

Was Rick saying what she thought he was saying? ''You mean—we're going to announce it to our friends? Just as if it were the truth?''

Shrugging, he squeezed her hand. ''I can't see any other way. But what the heck,'' he added with a mischievous grin, ''it'll be fun to lay my engagement on the typing pool. Half of them are in love with me, you know.''

Priscilla made a disgusted sound. ''I'm sure, Rick. And this news will break every one of their hearts.''

''I don't think the impact will be that dramatic, but it should liven up the place.''

''You know I think you're actually beginning to enjoy this,'' Priscilla muttered.

''I've never been engaged before. Kinda gives me a feeling of—well—belonging,'' he said rather expressively.

She stared at him. ''Belonging? Rick, this is pretend. Like when you were a little boy and you played Cowboys-and-Indians.''

He shook his head. ''I always played Cops-and-Robbers and pretended to be Sam Spade.''

She laughed in spite of everything. ''Complete with dames in distress, no doubt.''

"I've always liked women," he defended.

"Well, that's definitely going to have to stop," she said primly.

His steps halted so quickly that Priscilla nearly fell face-forward on the concrete. If Rick hadn't been holding on to her hand, she would have.

"Did I hear right?" he asked aghast. "Does this mean I can't date?"

Priscilla actually stamped her foot. A moment ago he'd been talking about feelings of belonging, and now he was worried about dating! She wished she had enough muscle to actually throttle him. "Rick! The past few minutes you've been preaching about how we had to play this thing to the hilt. I'm sure Mother would love hearing about her future son-in-law playing around."

"I'd be discreet."

"I knew you were the wrong man. Just consider our short-lived engagement broken!" she hissed, quickly stalking ahead of him.

Rick stared after her. "Priscilla, you can't mean that!"

The wounded sound in his voice made her even angrier, and she hastened her steps. "I do mean it," she tossed over her shoulder. "You're not the right man. I could never marry anyone with such shallow standards."

"But you're not going to marry me," he reasoned, trotting to catch up to her.

"Thank God," she quipped.

Disappointment flooded through Rick. He didn't know why, they'd only been going to pretend to be engaged, he told himself. But he'd been looking forward to it in some strange way. And now she was saying it was all over. He hadn't felt this much pain even when that blonde from Beaumont had cracked a bottle of champagne over his head. "Priscilla, you're acting foolish. You have to use me. I'm the only man available."

Priscilla stopped on the sidewalk, looking at him with hurt brown eyes. "You don't even think enough of me to—to forgo a woman for a week. One week! I thought you were my friend, Rick."

"I am, sugar. I am." Moving close to her, he lifted his hands and framed her face with his palms. "And you can count on me. I won't even look at another woman. I promise," he said with soft persuasion.

The touch of his hands on her face melted all her resistance. Gazing into his blue, blue eyes, she wondered how it would be if Rick really did love her, really did want to marry her. The idea made her virtually tremble. "Your promises are always broken."

A slow smile spread across his mouth. "I bought you two packs of root beer."

"I don't believe it," she said, wishing he'd take his hands away. She was feeling flushed and flustered. If Rick knew that he was affecting her in this way, he'd be amused and she'd be horribly embarrassed.

"I'll prove it when we get back home. They're on the front seat of my car."

Had he actually gone out of his way to buy her root beer? He never had before. "You—bought root beer?"

"Most women prefer diamonds, but I know where your tastes lie," he said, caressing her soft cheeks with his thumbs. "So don't you think that entitles me to be your intended?"

Her intended, she thought, a funny little feeling curling in the pit of her stomach. "You're sounding old-fashioned Rick. What would all your girlfriends say?"

The feigned look of innocence on his face wasn't lost to Priscilla, even though darkness was rapidly falling over them and the ocean.

"What girlfriends? I'm an engaged man."

"For a week," she said, more as a reminder to herself than to him.

His perfectly chiseled mouth curled up into a smile just before he leaned down and pressed it to Priscilla's warm, moist one.

Rick had intended to make the caress quick and casual, but she tasted so unexpectedly sweet that he forgot himself. Moments began to pass as he kissed her, not as a friend but as a lover.

When it was finally over and he stepped back from her, Priscilla was in a state of shock. Her hand flew to her hot mouth as she stared up at him.

''What—why did you do that?''

Rick couldn't answer. Right at this moment, he didn't know the answer. He only knew that Priscilla had felt warm and wonderful in his arms. The realization stunned him as much as the kiss had surprised her.

Careful, Rick, he told himself. This game of pretense might prove to be the most dangerous game you've ever played.

Chapter Four

"Well, you don't have to make it sound like a dreaded chore," Rick retorted.

Feeling the need to keep things light, Priscilla made a face at him. "I'm not in the habit of kissing anyone. Especially not you. I need time to adjust."

He took her arm, urging her along in the direction of home. "From what you've told me, there's hardly any time before your mother will be here. Before that happens you need to get that look."

Priscilla glanced warily up at him. "That look? Am I supposed to know what that means?"

His mouth twisted with faint mockery. "Your mother is expecting to find you madly in love—with me. She should be able to read it on your face."

Priscilla shook her head in complete exasperation. "And how do you expect me to do that? I've never been in love in my life. Have you?"

It was dark now. Every so often the two of them passed beneath a street lamp. As the next pool of light approached, Priscilla took the opportunity to glance up at Rick in an effort to read his face, and found it marred by a tiny frown.

Rick was thinking back through the many girlfriends he'd had over the years. He couldn't really say he'd been in love with any one of them. He'd been highly attracted at times, but never in love. Love was a risky, and from all he'd seen a painful, thing. A thing he most definitely wanted to avoid. "No. I haven't."

"Then how would you know about that look?"

Rick's expression grew wicked and his blue eyes gleamed back at her. "I said I hadn't been in love, I didn't say anyone hadn't been in love with me."

Priscilla closed her eyes and shook her head. "Mere words couldn't describe your conceit, Rick."

He made a tsk-ing noise with his tongue. "That's not conceit, Pris. That's experience."

"I'll just bet," she said dryly.

Rick pulled her to a stop and Priscilla turned to face him. Rick put his hand under her chin and lifted her face up to his. Chuckling, he said,

"Okay, let's see how well you do. Give me a loving look."

"Rick! You're crazy. We're outside. Anyone could see us."

Rick rolled his eyes. "Pris, I said a loving look, that doesn't mean jump into my arms. Besides, it's dark, and," he glanced back over their shoulders, "there's no one around, anyway."

"Still, this is ridiculous. I can't."

"Come on, Priscilla. Try," he urged.

"You give me one first, and then I'll know more of what's expected of me," she countered primly.

Rick loosened his hold on her chin and slid his forefinger lightly down the side of her throat. Her skin was incredibly soft, just the way her lips had been when he'd kissed her. The urge to kiss her again rose up inside him, taking him by complete surprise.

Priscilla closely studied Rick's expression, trying her best to keep her mind on learning instead of feeling. But with Rick's finger doing a dance of its own against her throat, all she could do was wonder if she was heading toward double trouble.

"You don't look like you're looking at a fiancé, Rick. You look like you're seeing a ghost, or some kind of alien," Priscilla said with disappointment.

Rick jerked his drifting thoughts back together. "That's not my 'look' yet. I'm concentrating, so I can get it right."

"If you have to concentrate about it, Mother will certainly know it isn't natural," Priscilla said with a groan.

"Well, at least I'm trying. You won't even attempt that," Rick countered impatiently.

"All right. I can do it. Anybody can act if they put their mind to it," she said with conviction.

Shaking back her hair, she put her hands on his shoulders and did her best to remember how Scarlett looked at Rhett Butler when she'd wanted him to kiss her.

Rick was taken by surprise as Priscilla's head fell limply back and her eyes took on a dreamy, come-hither expression. Instinctively his hands spanned the back of her waist and before he realized what he was doing he had bent his head down to her. "Priscilla," he breathed, "you look—"

"Like I'm in love?" she asked brightly, quickly pushing away from him.

Muddled, Rick shook his head to clear his senses. For a moment, there, he'd thought it was the real thing on her face. For a moment he'd wanted it to be real! Lord, wouldn't Priscilla laugh if she knew that, he thought. "Er—well, it was pretty good," he told her a bit reluctantly. He didn't want to say more and have her guessing just how fooled he'd been by that look in her eyes.

Unaware of his reaction to her, Priscilla smiled

happily. "Oh, I'm glad you thought so. Maybe this won't be quite as hard as I thought."

Rick grabbed her by the arm and began leading her in the direction of home. "I think we've had enough practice for tonight. I have a stack of paperwork waiting on me."

"Oh, yes, I'd forgotten you have work to do. I'm sorry, Rick. I've been taking up your time with my problem." She hugged his arm affectionately against her as they walked. "But when this is all over I truly will make it up to you somehow. I promise."

Rick's sidelong glance was full of wry skepticism. "And how do you propose to do that?"

She gave him a proper look. "Well, it won't be with a naked girl breaking out of a cake. But I'll think of something—nice."

Rick threw back his head and howled. "Oh, my precious Priscilla, life would be so boring without you."

And it would be boring without you, Rick, she thought. Boring and empty.

The idea kept Priscilla in quiet contemplation as they walked the remaining distance back to the beach house. Walks wouldn't be nearly as enjoyable if she didn't have Rick strolling beside her, his strong arm to hang onto. And what would dinner be like, night after night, without Rick sitting across the table from her, teasing her, pestering her, talking over his day with her?

"Rick, you've never really told me why you don't want to get married. Why not?"

By now they'd reached the house. Rick glanced at her as they started toward the staircase that would carry them up to their respective apartments. "Is this a trick question?" he asked.

She frowned at him. "A trick question? What could be tricky about it?"

He shrugged, feeling far more uncomfortable than he wanted Priscilla to know. Not that he tried to hide things from her—God knew they'd talked about any and everything since they'd become friends. But he'd always skirted around the issue of marriage. "You know how you teachers are. You always want to make at least one question tricky, just so it would be impossible to score a hundred."

She made an impatient sound under her breath. "And do you always want to make a perfect score?"

He grinned at her. "You've got it, Priscilla."

She was clearly disappointed. "The answer to my question? That's it?"

"That's it," he said easily and began to mount the steps.

Priscilla quickly followed. "So, you don't want to get married because you're afraid you wouldn't be a perfect husband, or wouldn't have the perfect marriage?''

Rick stopped long enough to answer. ''After growing up with parents who continually hurt each other, I know there isn't such a thing as a perfect marriage.''

Priscilla had never seen Rick pessimistic about anything until now, and it surprised her greatly. Oh, she'd known he was a confirmed bachelor by choice, but she hadn't guessed his views about marriage went so deep. She continued to follow him up the stairs. ''I don't remember you saying your parents were divorced.''

Now at the top, Rick stopped again, this time folding his arms and leaning against the banister of the sun deck. ''My parents were married right up until the time my mother passed away. But in my opinion they should have divorced long before that.'' Sighing, he shook is head. ''They stayed together because of me. Because they thought it was what I wanted and needed. And I feel very guilty because of that. They would have been much happier apart.''

Priscilla could understand that. Many times she'd thought her parents would have been happier if she hadn't come along in their life. Tracie had been planned, wanted. Priscilla had merely been a late-in-life accident. Yet she couldn't bear to think of Rick feeling guilty or melancholy about anything. "That's nonsense. I'm sure that deep down they stayed together because they loved each other."

Rick's lips took on a cynical twist. "If that's love, I'm certain I don't ever want to find myself in that condition."

A few inches from him, Priscilla propped her hip against the banister and studied his glum expression. "Rick, I hate hearing you talk like this. It's—it's unhealthy."

He smiled vaguely at her words, then reached over and clasped her hand in his. "I've never had anyone worry about my welfare like you, Pris. I wonder why that is?"

She felt her cheeks grow warm, even though the ocean breeze was cool against her face. "If I don't watch out for you, I'll end up with a different neighbor and I've just now broken you in."

He laughed, and then they both went quiet for a while. Priscilla didn't mind. Being with Rick was special, even when they weren't talking or laughing. To have him just holding her hand in the darkness was a sweet reassurance for Priscilla.

"Rick, do you ever imagine yourself as old?" she asked.

"Sometimes. Why do you ask?"

She shrugged, then turned her head and looked out at the restless ocean. "Oh, I don't know. I guess it's this marriage thing and talk about having children. It would be sad to grow old without a husband or children.''

''What I'd call sad is not having a fat retirement check and a ticket to Las Vegas,'' Rick countered.

Priscilla scowled at him disapprovingly. ''You don't even like gambling.''

With a soft chuckle, Rick patted her hand. ''Well, there's always the show girls.''

''Okay, nasty boy, that takes care of your future. But I have no interest in show girls.''

He grinned impishly down at her serious little face. ''You'll always have your books. Your quiet evening with Yeats.''

Yes, but could Yeats talk back, make her laugh or hold her hand? she thought a bit dismally. ''That's not my idea of something to look forward to,'' she muttered. ''And I meant it earlier, when I said I was seriously going to start looking for a man.''

A frown suddenly marred Rick's handsome face. ''Priscilla, you're still very young. Don't you think you're getting carried away with all this?''

Even though in the past Rick had often encouraged Priscilla to date, the idea of her looking for a life mate bothered him nore than he cared to admit. She was a babe in the woods. He couldn't bear to think of some man taking advantage of her sweetness, her innocence. He couldn't bear to think she might wind up in the kind of unhappy marriage his own mother had had.

Priscilla shook her head. As she did so, the breeze caught her hair, tangling it across her eyes. She pulled her hand from his in order to reach up and push the wayward strands from her vision. "You won't always be here, Rick. And right now, when I look thirty years down the road—Williard almost looks good!"

"Priscilla! My God, I think I'll whack you across the bottom if you say his name again." Rick took her by the shoulders and pushed her toward the house. "Go to bed. It's almost nine-thirty. If you're not in bed by ten, you won't be worth two cents tomorrow."

"You're right, Rick," she agreed glumly. "There's nothing I can do about any of this tonight, anyway. I'll see you tomorrow when you get home from work."

Nodding, he smiled encouragingly. "It's all going to work out, sugar. Don't worry."

She gave him a little wave, then disappeared around the corner of the deck to enter her side of the duplex. Rick slowly entered his own apartment and plopped down on the couch.

Across the cluttered room his packed briefcase lay on a small desk, waiting for him to work. But tonight his mind was far away from work. Priscilla's questions about marriage were still pestering him. She'd made him look back at his life, at the misery his parents had gone through as they'd hung onto an unhappy marriage. From the time Rick had become a teenager, he'd vowed to never get married, never fall in love. And, so far, avoiding those two things had kept his life very happy. Now Priscilla was trying to tell him, and herself, that life without those two things would be empty. He couldn't believe that. And this thing with Priscilla's parents was only making her want to believe it, he tried to reason.

Frustrated, Rick leaned back against the couch and raked his fingers through his hair. No one wanted to think of himself as old, and Rick was only thirty. Why should he sit around worrying about his golden years? he asked himself.

Nearly two hours later Rick was sitting at the kitchen table, absently tapping a pencil against a stack of reports. A cup of cold coffee stood at his elbow and a faraway look was on his face.

Tomorrow a group of businessmen was coming in from New Mexico to talk over a gas purchase. If he was unable to quote the right facts and figures to them, the deal would probably fly right out the window. But every time Rick attempted to read the reports, he kept envisioning Priscilla ten years from now, living a boring life with wimpy Williard. Instead of wine, candlelight and wild, wanton sex on the kitchen floor, she would be carrying a pipe and slippers to a math teacher who cleaned his bird cage for excitement!

The image was sickening to Rick and he tossed down his pencil before he gave in to the urge to break it. He had to quit thinking like this, he told himself, massaging his throbbing temples. Just because he'd gotten engaged to her tonight didn't mean he was responsible for her future.

Damn, Rick, a little voice inside him scolded. You're really losing it. This is only a pretend engagement, and as for Priscilla finding a real husband, that's none of your business. Like hell, he said to the voice. She's my friend. I can't let her make a mistake, just because she feels an unreasonable need to please her parents.

The whole thing left him feeling the need for a drink. Preferably a stiff Scotch. But he didn't keep alcohol around the place. Unless it was beer.

Rising from the table, Rick jerked open the refrigerator door only to find the shelves were practically empty. Priscilla usually did all the cooking, so he didn't bother buying groceries until she told him it was his turn. Tonight he couldn't even find a can of soda.

The root beer! He'd left it on the front seat of the car. In less than two seconds he was out the door and bounding down the steps.

* * *

Groaning tiredly, Priscilla rolled onto her stomach and buried her face deeper into the pillow. For the past two hours she'd tried her best to fall asleep. At least a million sheep had jumped over her bed. Now she was in a rowboat drifting on a calm lake. The years were rolling by her, but still she could see Rick. Was that a blackjack table he was standing at? His blond hair was streaked with gray, instead of sunshine. There were also wrinkles on his face, yet he was still a very handsome man. Beside him a young blonde hung on his arm, batted her eyelashes up at him, and called him Sugar Daddy.

Priscilla bolted straight up in the bed. Her heart was pounding in her chest as she scanned the dark bedroom and tried to orient herself.

Groggily, she noticed a light was on in the kitchen. Throwing back the covers, she stumbled toward it.

"Rick! Is that you?" she asked, leaning against the doorjamb.

"Pris! I thought you were asleep," he said with surprise, as he pushed shut the refrigerator door.

With one hand over her eyes, she shook her head. "I was. At least I think I was. I don't know." She dropped her hand and moved into the room. "Oh, Rick, I had the most horrible vision of you."

As Priscilla groped her way into a chair, Rick noticed she wasn't wearing Mickey tonight. Instead it was a midnight blue nightshirt that struck her mid-calf, and the way the silky material clung to her curves was giving him a vision of his own.

"Really?" he asked curiously.

She looked up at him. "You know how we were talking about thirty years from now? Well, I think I just saw you in the future."

"Hmm," he said, "that's funny, because I saw you, too. Earlier, when I was trying to work."

Priscilla's expression was suddenly wary. "Was it bad?" she wanted to know.

He took the chair across from her. "Terrible," he said grimly, as he imagined wimpy Williard giving Priscilla a chaste kiss on the cheek.

Priscilla shook her head. "It couldn't have been as bad as mine."

"I can't imagine anything as bad as what I saw," he said wearily.

"Oh. Was I dead or something?" Priscilla asked curiously.

Rick's lips formed a stern line. "You might as well have been. You were with Williard."

Priscilla groaned, and Rick asked, "So what about me?"

Priscilla clasped her hands on the tabletop and leaned toward him. "You were at a gaming table and a young, blond—" she had to force herself to spit the last of it out "—gold digger was on your arm."

His eyebrows lifted dryly. "You call that bad?"

She gave him an angry look. "Of course it was bad! It meant—well, it meant you'd gone through your whole life un-unloved."

"And that bothers you?" he asked softly, the humor fading from his face.

"Of course it does. You're my dearest friend. I want you to be happy."

"As I do you, Pris."

There was something soft, something caring in Rick's voice that Priscilla had never heard before. It surprised her almost as much as his kiss had earlier this evening. She'd liked that kiss. Liked it entirely too much, if she was totally honest with herself. Still, the idea that he might kiss her again while her mother was around sent a shiver of anticipation through her.

Thinking she should get her thoughts on safer ground, she asked, "What are you doing in here, anyway? Stealing my root beer?"

Feigning a look of hurt, Rick rose to his feet. "Is that any way to talk to your new fiancé? Especially when I just restocked your fridge."

Priscilla jumped from her chair and hurried over to the refrigerator. Two six-packs minus one can were resting on the top shelf. At the sight of them, a warm feeling went through Priscilla. "How sweet of you, Rick. But what happened to that one can?"

She turned around to see he was standing right behind her. A sheepish expression was on his face as he pointed toward the cabinet counter and the single unopened can sitting there. "I was thirsty for something besides coffee," he confessed. "So now that you've caught me, why don't we share it? We haven't toasted our engagement yet, anyway."

"People don't toast a lie," Priscilla said wearily.

"Oh come on, sugar, it isn't a lie. It's just a little pretense."

"Does that make it any more justified?"

Rick shook his head with disbelief as he turned to the cabinets. "Priscilla, are you forgetting this was your idea? Remember, I was the one who advised you to call your mother and tell her the truth."

Releasing a long breath, she reached up and pressed the heels of her palms against her temples. "Yes, I know," she conceded. "But it was only because—because I just couldn't let her down. She sounded so—happy, so proud of me."

Rick reached up and pulled down two glasses, then went to the fridge for ice. "Then you shouldn't feel badly about anything. You're doing what you think is best. Besides, the whole thing is going to be fun."

Amazed, Priscilla watched him pop the top of the soda can and pour it over the ice. "Fun? You are out of your mind, Rick. I've always suspected it. Now I know it.''

Chuckling, he turned and handed her one of the glasses. ''I know the word is a foreign one to you, Pris. But given time, you might get the hang of it.''

She gave him a dreary smile. ''Rick, do you ever have a serious moment? Intentionally, that is.''

''Of course, I do. I'm serious right now.'' He drew closer and with a wicked grin on his face, clinked his glass against hers. ''To us, sugar. May we both get what we want out of life.''

Her brown eyes leveled on his blue ones and her heart thumped strangely as she echoed his words. ''To us.''

Chapter Five

It was raining in downtown Houston the next day, when Rick left his office building and drove to a nearby jeweler.

Steam rose from the streets as the cool rain hit the hot asphalt. It often rained in Houston, but Rick was never depressed by it. Certainly he wasn't today. The meeting with the New Mexican people had gone well. Added to that, he'd spent the remainder of the morning receiving good wishes from his co-workers on his engagement. And naturally the typing-pool grapevine had buzzed with the news. Rick had enjoyed every minute of it.

He'd been right last night, when he'd told Priscilla the whole thing was going to be fun. He liked the idea of having people think he was adored and

cherished by one certain woman. He liked the
sense of attachment and belonging an engagement
signified. He just didn't like what came afterward.
To Rick, pain and marriage were synonymous.
And pain wasn't on his list of likes. But this was
a pretend engagement, therefore a safe one.

Rick found a parking spot as near to the jewelry
store as possible, then made a dash for the en-
trance. Even so his white shirt was splotched with
rain as he opened the glass door. He was attempt-
ing to brush the beads of moisture from his hair
when a young saleswoman walked up to him.

"Can I help you, sir?"

Rick smiled at the brunette. "I want to buy an
engagement ring."

The young woman nodded, then indicated for
Rick to follow her across the plush carpeting of the
display room. "Did you have anything specific in
mind?" she asked as she slipped behind a glass
counter.

Rick glanced around at the quiet shoppers min-
gling through the store and asked himself what he
was doing here. You're here to buy Priscilla a ring,
a real ring, a silent voice growled back at him. "I
hadn't really thought about it," he lied to the saleslady.

In truth, Rick had thought about it all morning
and he'd come to the conclusion that he wasn't
about to let Priscilla wear a fake stone. She was

worthy of more than that. Besides, the ring was suppose to signify the bond between them. He wanted Priscilla's mother to find a dazzling diamond on her daughter's finger.

The woman gave him an understanding smile. "Perhaps you could tell me something about your fiancée and I could make a few suggestions."

She pulled a large tray of rings from beneath the counter and placed it in front of Rick. "Does your fiancée work?"

"She's a schoolteacher. Elementary," Rick added. "She's very dedicated and good at it, too."

Smiling, the saleslady nodded as though she was used to dealing with proud fiancés. "Is she the dress-up sort? Or does she like things casual?"

Rick could probably count on one hand the times he'd seen Priscilla really dressed up. But, then, she didn't have many opportunities for things like that. Once she'd gone to the ballet in Houston with one of her girlfriends. It was the first time Rick had seen Priscilla in formal clothes. Her dress had been mauve, with a little see-through jacket that showed the tiny straps on her shoulders. She'd looked very pretty, and he remembered telling her she should dress up and go out more. "Well, she's mostly casual. But nice things look good on her, too. You know what I mean?"

The young woman gave Rick an appreciative

glance. "Yes, I do. Maybe she'd like something like this?"

Rick glanced at the ring she pointed to, then shook his head. "It's nice, but a bit too showy."

"Are her hands small or large?"

The corners of Rick's mouth tilted upward as he thought of Priscilla's little brown hands. She always left the nails just over the edge of her fingertips and painted them pink or coral. Once she'd done them in red and Rick had teased her about it. Later he was sorry he had, because she'd never worn red again after that. And Rick liked red, especially on Priscilla.

"Small, plump and very pretty. Size five and a half, to be exact."

"She sounds like a solitaire woman to me."

Rick cut his eyes up at the sales woman. More than you can imagine, he felt like telling her. "I think I like this one," Rick said, pointing out a marquise-shaped stone set in white gold.

"That one is lovely. It's also one of our more expensive rings. But you look like a man who appreciates a good woman," she told him. "And I'm sure your wife-to-be deserves it."

Of course she deserved it, Rick thought. Priscilla was a wonderful person. She'd been his dearest, closest friend since he'd moved to Galveston Island. When he'd run into rough spots, she'd always been there to help him through them. He couldn't imagine life without Priscilla somewhere in it. "Yes, she does. So I'll take it. Can you size it for me this afternoon?"

That evening on his way home Rick kept glancing down at the velvet jewel box on the seat beside him. He'd been extravagant. He'd been crazy! Priscilla was expecting a piece of junk jewelry and he'd bought a diamond that had cost enough to stagger even him. Now she was going to expect a receipt for the thing. He'd simply have to make up an excuse that he'd lost it, he decided. If Priscilla found out the rock was real she'd go into a tailspin. And God only knew how he could explain it to her. He couldn't even explain his actions to himself.

But, damn it, he thought, as he maneuvered his car through the congested traffic on Highway 45. Priscilla deserved the best, whether their engagement was real or not. And the ring would pay her back for all those meals she'd cooked for him, he reasoned with himself.

Feeling he'd justified his behavior, Rick settled his arm across the back of the seat and smiled like a sleepy cat. He couldn't wait to see Priscilla's face when he gave her the ring.

Priscilla wasn't in the mood to prepare supper. Most of her classes had been unruly, as they often were when school was nearing its final days. Priscilla couldn't blame the children for wanting school to be over for the summer, she was ready for a rest herself, but today she'd hardly been able to concentrate, much less deal with disruptive students.

For some odd reason Rick had continually stayed in her thoughts. What he was doing for her was—well, it was more than anyone had ever done for her. And that kiss he'd given her. She couldn't forget how those few moments in his arms she'd felt like a real woman. Priscilla knew it wasn't good to think about such a thing. Rick was a playboy and he'd only been playing with her. Just because they were pretending to be engaged didn't mean she could allow her feelings for him to grow into anything more than the feelings of a friend. Yet a part of her wasn't quite heeding that warning.

She was placing pasta and meatballs on the table when she heard Rick whistling as he climbed the stairs. Her heart lifted at the sound and she smiled to herself as she imagined the look on his face when he saw she'd prepared his favorite meal.

Walking over to the door connecting their apartments, Priscilla opened it and stuck her head through. "Rick, supper is ready," she called out to him.

"I'll be right there, Pris," he answered from

somewhere in the other part of the house. "And don't pour tea. I've brought us a bottle of wine."

"Wine?" she echoed, loud enough for him to hear.

"Yeah. I thought we'd get drunk and go get our names tattooed on each other."

Rolling her eyes at his nonsense, she said, "I'm sure you've already picked out certain parts of our anatomies for the occasion."

She could hear him laughing as he moved through the house. "Naturally. Want to hear where yours is?"

He walked into the kitchen, holding up the bottle of wine. He grinned impishly at Priscilla's indignant expression.

"No, thank you. I'd rather eat," she told him, tossing her head and turning back to her own kitchen.

Rick followed, rolling up the sleeves of his white shirt as he did. "Mmm. Do I smell your wonderful meatballs?"

Priscilla had never realized until now how much pleasing Rick pleased her. "You do," she said, reaching up and pulling down two wineglasses from the cabinet.

"Sugar, you do know how to make me happy."

Something always went soft in her when Rick called her sugar, but tonight the feeling was even stronger.

"Got a corkscrew?" he asked, coming up behind her.

She turned her head and her face almost collided with his. The first thing her eyes focused on was his mouth, which was a mistake because it reminded her once again of that kiss. She wished he'd never done it! No, she didn't wish that, her mind swiftly countered. It had been too delicious to wish away. But she was like a dieter eyeing a fudge brownie. Rick was a no-no.

"Yes, just—" she began.

Before she could turn back away from him, Rick leaned forward and kissed her on the cheek. "Mmm. You smell like jasmine," he mused. "Nice, Priscilla. You didn't wear that for wimpy Williard, did you?"

Frowning, she moved away from him and jerked open a cabinet drawer. "I only saw Williard in passing today," she muttered in a flustered voice. "Anyway, it wouldn't be any of your business if I did wear it for Williard. Which I didn't," she tacked on.

He took the corkscrew from her and stabbed the middle of the cork. "Of course it's my business. You're my betrothed. I don't want another man considering you his flower."

Priscilla shook her head with mocking disbelief. "Cut the bull, Rick. We both know if it weren't for this engagement thing, you'd be dialing one of those numbers in your little black book right now. And an hour from now you'd be hightailing it out of here with some fluffhead. And you wouldn't care what I smelled like!''

Rick laughed as he worked the corkscrew and eyed her flushed cheeks. "Why, Pris, you make me sound terrible, and I'm not. I was the one who suggested this. And who else would bring you wine for dinner and a—surprise," he added with a gleam in his eye.

Priscilla arched a brow at him. "A surprise? What is it?"

He put a hand on her shoulder and guided her to the table. "Later, sugar. Now sit and I'll pour."

Priscilla watched him fill the glasses with wry speculation. "Did you tell your co-workers that you're getting married?" she asked.

"Uh-huh. What about you?"

Priscilla tossed back her silky brown hair and Rick watched it slide back into place against her neck.

"Yes. I think the whole school was in a state of shock. But I guess they'll be just as shocked when I return in the fall unengaged."

"I've already had several cigars given to me," Rick continued. "And one of the senior execs wants us to name our firstborn after him."

"What's his name?"

"Winfred."

Priscilla couldn't help but burst out laughing. "Can't you see us with a son named Winfred?" she said with a giggle. Then suddenly her cheeks flamed and she went still and quiet.

"What's wrong?"

Priscilla shook her head. "Oh, I—just thought of how ridiculous that sounded. You and I with a child."

Rick grimaced, then shrugged. "Well, I'd like to think I could sire a child. Don't you like to think you could conceive one?"

Her eyes lifted up to his. "I—yes, I suppose so. But us—together. The idea is laughable."

She wasn't laughing, but Rick didn't notice that. He was too busy wondering about the pang of disappointment he was suddenly experiencing. It was crazy, he thought. He didn't want or need children in his life! He was a tried-and-true bachelor.

"Rick, the meatballs are getting cold. Aren't you going to sit down?"

"What—?" Shaking away his thoughts, he glanced down at her.

"I'm waiting for you to sit," she said patiently.

Glancing down at the table, he said, "Just a minute. We must have candles," he said, quickly heading back to his kitchen.

Priscilla opened her mouth to question him, but he was gone before she had a chance. But it was only a matter of seconds before he returned with a couple of tall candles in a pair of silver holders.

"Rick Lowrimore, if you've used those candles for your—girlfriends, I don't want them on my table!"

"Pris!" he scolded. "I bought these for Christmas. Can't you tell?"

She eyed them warily and had to concede they were at least red. "It's only dusk. There's no need for candles."

Rick ignored her as he struck a match and lighted both wicks, then reached to switch off the overhead light. "This is a special occasion."

"It is?"

The room dimmed. She scooted her chair forward and watched the candles glow to life. Rick watched her.

"We're celebrating our engagement," he said with conviction.

"But—"

"No buts. This may be the only time either one of us is ever engaged. We need to make the most of it." There was such an endearing expression on his good-looking face that Priscilla found herself smiling at him. She'd never been able to resist Rick when he was being sweet.

"Whatever you say, dear Rick."

After the vision he'd had last night, he figured he could at least give Priscilla one night of wine and candlelight. As far as the wild, wanton sex on the kitchen floor, Rick didn't think she was ready for that. The idea had him looking across the candlelight at her sweet face. Priscilla was a lovely woman, with her smooth, golden skin and sexy brown eyes. Her full curves would constantly remind a man he was a man. Oh, yes, he realized with sharp surprise, he could easily picture himself making love to Priscilla.

They filled their plates and began to eat. By the time they'd reached the dessert stage, the sun had disappeared completely and the kitchen had grown dark except for the twin candles. Rick refilled their wineglasses, then brought out the small jewelry box.

Seeing it, Priscilla realized she'd forgotten that Rick had planned to pick up a ring today. "You didn't have to get a special box for it, Rick. Did you bring the receipt with you?"

Averting his gaze from hers, Rick reached for his wineglass. He was nervous! Damn it, he'd never been nervous in his life. "Er—no, I left it at the office."

"Well, please remember to bring it home so I can reimburse you."

Rick opened the box and held it over for her to see. "What do you think?"

Priscilla's eyes grew wide, then narrow. "Gosh,

if I didn't know better, I'd believe it was real. It's very pretty, Rick.''

Pretty! He'd just written a check that was going to shrivel his bank account and she could only come up with pretty! He pulled the ring from its nest and tried to remind himself that Priscilla believed she was looking at a fake.

''Here, let's put it on and see how it looks.'' He reached for her hand and slid the ring onto her third finger.

A strange feeling coursed through Priscilla as his warm fingers gently held hers. She hadn't expected any of this from him. It was almost as if they were doing the traditional things that a real couple would do. ''I guess you can view all this as practice,'' she tried to joke.

''Priscilla, I can't see me doing this to any other woman but you.''

Taken by surprise by his words, her eyes flew from their hands up to his face. If it hadn't been so dark in the room, she would have sworn he was blushing.

''I mean—well, I don't ever intend getting engaged and you're the only woman who understands that,'' he tried to explain himself.

Priscilla studied his face as she tried to decide whether to be relieved or disappointed. ''I see,'' she murmured, then looked down at the ring on her finger. It was really dazzling, even if it was a fake, she thought.

"Do you like the ring?"

She couldn't imagine why it should be so important to him when the whole thing was just a sham.

"I like it very much. I'm sure Mother and all my friends will be duly impressed."

"So will you show it off tomorrow?" He didn't know why that would matter to him, but it did.

Smiling, she pulled her hand from his. "I'll show it all over school and everyone will think my fiancé spent a fortune on me. That's almost sinful, you know it?"

Oh, he knew it all right. Rick passed a weary hand over his tousled hair. "Almost," he said, trying his best to sound innocent.

"Ready for dessert?" she asked, rising quickly from her chair.

"You made dessert, too? Priscilla, you're spoiling me."

"You're already spoiled," she told him as she went over to the cabinet. "But since you're being so sweet about helping me out, I thought you deserved a little extra."

She carried two saucers back to the table. On them were squares of rich cheesecake topped with a glaze of blueberries. Rick groaned with pleasure. "You know the way to my heart, Pris."

Priscilla knew better than that. From what he'd told her he kept his heart very guarded, and a woman like herself would never get near it. Not even with cheesecake.

She took her seat again and picked up her fork. "I truly am grateful to you, Rick." With her free hand she reached over and touched his forearm. "It means very much to me."

Rick breathed deeply as he watched the candlelight flicker across her face. He'd never been able to figure out why he'd always felt so close to Priscilla. From the first day he'd met her, he'd felt completely in tune with her. And that was completely unexplainable because they were nothing alike. Maybe it was because she was so unlike the women he dated that he found her so refreshing. Whatever the case, Rick felt that something had changed between them the past two days. He didn't know why, or exactly what, but it had. And the idea scared him. They had something special between them. He didn't want anything to ruin it. So why did he keep getting the urge to lean across the table and kiss her?

Leaning forward he took hold of her hand. At once, he felt something stir inside him at the feel of her soft fingers, and he moved even closer. "You truly are welcome, sugar," he murmured.

Priscilla's heart fluttered beneath her breast. What was he doing, and why did he have that strange look in his eyes? she wondered. Before she could come up with an answer, his lips had moved over hers. Softly, gently, they teased and tasted.

Without knowing it, her eyes closed, her fingers gripped his, and the room began to spin around them.

Priscilla had never been kissed like this. She'd never felt like this. She wanted to go on kissing Rick forever.

Kissing Rick! Her spinning senses suddenly came to a screeching halt. This couldn't happen. This wasn't in the game plan.

She jerked back from him so quickly that Rick nearly fell face-forward in his cheesecake.

"Priscilla—"

In seconds she was out of her chair and on her feet. "Rick, you know I'm not into kissing men! Why did you have to go and do that?" she asked, her voice flustered. Yet the agitation was directed at herself, not at him.

Why had he? Rick asked himself. Because she'd looked so soft and vulnerable, he silently reasoned. Because he felt unreasonably protective of her, and because somewhere in some other part of him he wished that their engagement was real, and that he could kiss her as a real lover.

"Pris—don't get all heated up," he said, trying to make his voice light. Which was very difficult when he was feeling far more shaken than he had in a long time. "You know how I get carried away."

Carried away! Priscilla wondered what it would be like if he kissed her for real. The heat that was already in her cheeks grew even hotter.

"Rick, I'm not like the girls you—"

Before she could finish he was on his feet and beside her. "I know, Priscilla. I know. I forget myself at times, and you just looked so pretty in the candlelight." He pressed both her hands between his. "Come on, let's take our dessert out on the deck and see if there's any ships out tonight."

Confusion filled her face as she looked up at him. He thought she'd looked pretty? A man like Williard might think so. But not someone like Rick. Yet tonight, just for tonight, it would be nice to believe that he did.

"Rick, that kiss—"

"Look, Priscilla, we're both adults, and adults don't have to be in love to share a kiss."

The sudden hurt in her eyes made Rick want to kick himself, but he'd had to get out of this some way.

Nodding slowly she moved away from him and reached down for her cheesecake. "You always were telling me I'm stuffy and old-fasioned," she muttered.

Rick grimaced. "I only do that to get you to argue with me," he confessed.

She forced a smile on her face. "Well, it works." She moved away from him, blinking her eyes as she turned away from him. "Do you want to take coffee outside with us?"

At the moment Rick didn't want anything except for her to understand. "Priscilla, that kiss—"

She glanced over her shoulder at him. "Didn't mean a thing," she assured him. "It was just practice—something I can use when I'm looking for a real husband."

A real husband! He wanted to shout at her that he could be as real as any man. But that wouldn't make sense either, he thought miserably. Not when they were just friends.

Letting out a weary breath, he reached for his cheesecake. "You have coffee if you like. I think I'll have more wine." Like five or six more glasses, he muttered to himself. Grabbing the bottle he followed her out the door.

Chapter Six

"Priscilla, don't be nervous. There's nothing to be nervous about. You're going to pick up your mother, not the First Lady, for Pete's sake."

Priscilla recrossed her legs and glanced out the window of Rick's car. Hot, glorious sunshine was everywhere, and the palms lining the street rippled gently in the ocean breeze. It was a beautiful Saturday, but Priscilla was so keyed up a hurricane could have been going on and she wouldn't have noticed.

"You don't know Mother. If you did, you wouldn't be sounding so chipper," she told him.

His disbelieving chuckle had her turning her head toward him. If any other woman had been looking at Rick she would have probably been seeing the clean, angular lines of his face, the endearing way his blond hair curled about his head and the way his trim, muscular body filled out his olive twill slacks and white polo shirt.

However, Priscilla wasn't seeing any of that. She was seeing the man who knew her fears and her joys, her needs and wants. He was the person she turned to before anyone else. At the moment he was the only thing holding her together.

"Rick, promise me you won't back out of this thing."

Rick glanced at her as he maneuvered the car through the busy traffic. A scowl wrinkled his forehead. "Why should I back out?"

"Because—because Mother is so—well, she might get on your nerves and—"

"Mother-in-laws are supposed to get on your nerves," he assured her.

Sighing, she realized there was no way she could actually ready Rick for her mother. He'd just have to see for himself. "I'm so grateful to you for coming with me to meet her at the airport. You didn't have to, you know."

He grinned. "I know. But being a good guy just comes naturally to me."

"A week with Mother will no doubt prove just how good you are," she said.

Rick laughed lowly. "If I could put up with

Miss Towbridge for six weeks, I can put up with anything.''

''Who's Miss Towbridge? One of your groupies in the typing pool?''

''No, she was a replacement secretary when Helen went on maternity leave. Don't you remember? I think every evening for the whole six weeks I came home with a cracking headache.''

''Oh, yes, I do remember now. And if I remember right, the whole problem was the poor woman was sixty and overweight instead of blond and willowy.''

''Dear Priscilla, that is totally untrue. She was overbearing, not overweight. At any rate, don't worry about my part of the deal. You just make sure you keep that in-love look on your face and your side by mine. I promise you that your mother will leave here thoroughly convinced our engagement is the real thing.''

''I don't think we'll have to maul each other just to convince her,'' Priscilla said primly, averting her eyes from his by staring at the traffic ahead. Since that night in the kitchen when he'd given her the ring, Rick hadn't kissed her. At least not kissed her lips in that consuming mind-boggling way he had then. The few he'd given her on the cheeks had been hard enough to handle. Anything more and she was liable to do something crazy. Like swoon in his arms.

Rick sneaked a glance at Priscilla's profile. She was deep in thought, a frown puckering her brows. Rick wished he knew what she was tossing around in that head of hers. Was it him or her mother? Or was she simply worried about being physically affectionate with him? He hated to think so.

"There she is, Rick," Priscilla said, quickly pointing toward the baggage-claim area.

It was hard for Rick to tell if the little catch in Priscilla's voice was excitement or nervousness. "Priscilla, I hate to tell you this, but there's about twenty women in the direction you're pointing."

The airport terminal was clogged with weekend travelers. Priscilla and Rick dodged in and out of the crowd as they worked their way toward Gloria Parker.

"The one with the lime green suit," she explained. "Come on, before she wanders off and we lose her in the crowd." She urged Rick along with a hand on his arm.

"Mother! Over here!" she called as they approached the woman.

Gloria must have heard her daughter's voice for she turned and spotted them. With a little wave, she hurried toward the couple.

When she got within reach, she dropped her bags and threw her arms around Priscilla. "Oh, my little baby," she exclaimed. "It's so good to see you again!"

Priscilla returned her mother's hug, before turning to Rick with a shaky smile. "Mother, this is my fiancé, Rick Lowrimore."

Gloria Parker was a tall, slim woman with graying blond hair and keen brown eyes that swept up and down Rick as if he was a specimen under a microscope. Resisting the urge to squirm, Rick curled his arm around Priscilla's shoulders and smiled warmly at the woman. "It's nice to finally meet you, Mrs. Parker," Rick told the woman.

Gloria's eyes grew wide. "You're Priscilla's fiancé?" Totally dismayed, she looked from Rick to Priscilla and back again.

"Why, yes. I hope you approve," Rick replied.

Gloria made a flustered gesture with her hands. "Of course I approve! I just didn't—" She cocked a reproving brow at her daughter. "Priscilla! Why didn't you tell me he was so handsome!"

Priscilla's eyes darted from her mother up to Rick's face. "I—er, didn't I mention it?"

"No, you didn't." Her expression suddenly changing to one of pleasure, she reached for Rick's hand, drawing it into hers with an affectionate pat. "I can already see we're going to be wonderful friends. Aren't we, Rick?"

Rick looked pointedly down at Priscilla. Her face was blanched white except for two bright spots of color on her cheekbones. He tightened his hold on her shoulder. "If you're anything like Priscilla, then I know I'm going to love you, Mrs. Parker," he said, looking back at Gloria.

The older woman blushed with obvious pleasure. "Oh, please call me Gloria. After all, we'll be related soon."

Priscilla choked on a cough and quickly reached for her mother's cases. "Let's get out of this busy terminal," she said, giving Rick a silent signal with her eyes.

Rick took the cue and the cases. "Yes, I'm sure you're exhausted, Gloria, and Priscilla has made a lovely snack for us back at the house."

"I can't wait," Gloria said with a beaming smile. "It's so nice on the beach, and don't you love Priscilla's apartment? I know it's rather old, but the location is fabulous. Of course, Tracie thinks the furniture and the decorations need to be changed over completely. But I suppose that doesn't make any difference now that you're going to be married. You'll probably be moving to your house. You do own a house, don't you?" she asked Rick.

The wry disbelief on Rick's face was only noticed by Priscilla. "Er—no. Actually I live in the duplex next to Priscilla. Renting is much easier than taxes, maintenance and insurance."

Rick's explanation was waved away with a

ringed hand. "I understand you've been a bachelor up until now. But your ideas on security will change once you've walked down the aisle."

Priscilla wanted to groan. Rick wanted to laugh.

"We like where we live, don't we, darling?" he asked Priscilla, glancing down at her with a warm expression.

"I can't imagine living anywhere else," she agreed. "Beachfront property is very hard to come by."

"Yes, but it's not very appropriate for raising children. A toddler would be in the ocean before you could turn around."

Priscilla's brows lifted. Maybe Tracie hadn't been exaggerating. She hadn't been in her mother's presence for more than five minutes and she was already bringing up the subject of babies.

"Mother! Rick and I have only now become engaged. It's too early to be talking about children."

"Priscilla is wonderful with children," Rick spoke up before Priscilla could say more. "So I wouldn't worry about us living on the beach."

"Then you do plan on having children?" Gloria glanced hopefully from her daughter to her son-in-law-to-be.

Rick smiled indulgently. "At least two. In fact, Priscilla's maternal instinct was one of the first things that drew me to her."

He sounded so sincere, Priscilla figured he

couldn't have done better if he'd taken a year of acting lessons.

Gloria smiled proudly at her daughter. "Darling, however did you find a man like him?"

"I—uh, wasn't really looking. He just happened to find me."

Priscilla was relieved to see they'd finally made it to Rick's car. Hopefully, once she had her mother home and settled she would quit throwing out questions with the speed of a machine gun.

Rick deposited Gloria's bags in the trunk, then helped both women into the car, Priscilla up front by his side, and her mother in the back.

"Pris, darling, you can't imagine how excited I was when Tracie called with the news of your engagement. I must say at first it nearly floored me. I always thought Tracie would be the one to marry first."

Priscilla stared straight ahead at the congested traffic converging from the airport onto the main highway. "So did I," she practically muttered.

"Well, you rarely had boyfriends in high school and college. And the past few years you've shown no interest in men," Gloria explained.

That wasn't quite true, Priscilla thought. Rick had been in her life for a long time now. Perhaps that was why she hadn't gone looking for male companionship. She'd already had it in Rick.

"Your daughter doesn't tell everything," Rick

spoke up. "I was afraid if I didn't ask Priscilla to marry me when I did I was going to lose her to another man."

"Is that true, Priscilla? I didn't realize you'd been dating at all."

Priscilla wanted to clobber Rick. And he must have read it on her face because he reached across the seat and gently squeezed her hand.

"Well—er—" she began.

"Priscilla, don't try to get out of it," Rick interrupted. "You know you and Williard were getting close."

Priscilla's mouth dropped open in astonishment. Yet before she could force anything out of it, Rick pushed up her chin with his forefinger.

"Well, this is a surprise. You see," she directed at Rick, "my other daughter, Tracie, is the complete opposite of Priscilla. She's always been the one to draw men like flies. And naturally I thought she would be the one to marry first. Priscilla has— well, Priscilla was always quiet and studious, weren't you, darling?"

Priscilla's lips spread to a grim line. "Yes, you could say that. Fortunately Rick sees more to me than my outer wrapping."

Gloria made a scolding noise with her tongue. "Now, honey, I wasn't talking about the way you look. You're just as pretty as Tracie—it's just in a different way."

Sure, Priscilla thought dryly.

Feeling the need to shelter Priscilla from anything Gloria Parker might say, Rick reached over and drew her close to his side while keeping his arm around her shoulders.

"Priscilla has natural beauty. She hasn't had tucks or suctions or lifts. She isn't camouflaged with makeup or hair coloring. When I look at Priscilla, I know what I'm getting, the real thing," Rick said in a proud voice.

Priscilla knew that everything he was saying was merely for the benefit of her mother. Still, the unexpected tenderness in his voice brought a lump to her throat. She glanced up at him, unaware there was a soft quiver to her lower lip.

However Rick didn't miss it, or the silent thank-you in her eyes. Something in his chest tightened and he felt the fierce need to hold Priscilla in his arms, to assure her that he would always be there for her.

Priscilla turned her head slightly to glance back at her mother, then wished she hadn't. The woman was swelling with pride. And all because of Rick.

"You haven't shown your mother your ring, darling," Rick gently reminded.

"Oh, yes, Priscilla! My goodness I've been running on so I'd forgotten all about the ring," Gloria exclaimed while leaning up in the backseat toward her daughter.

Priscilla dangled her left hand over the seat and Gloria immediately snatched it up. "My, oh, my!" she breathed as she examined the ring on her daughter's finger. "That is a beautiful stone. Simply striking. Did you pick it out, Priscilla?"

Priscilla had never felt more like a fraud. Didn't her mother know a fake when she saw it? Don't be crazy, Priscilla, she silently scolded herself. Your mother isn't supposed to know the ring is a fake. She isn't supposed to know your engagement is a fake. Priscilla was suddenly exhausted.

"No, Rick surprised me with it," she murmured.

"Then you have excellent taste, Rick. And you must know Priscilla well, because the ring is perfect for her."

"Oh, I know Priscilla well," Rick said with a knowing smile. "Probably better than you do, Gloria."

By the time they reached the beach house, Priscilla's head was cracking. For the last ten minutes of the drive she'd remained quiet, content to let Rick handle her mother's incessant questions.

"I'll get your mother's cases, sugar," Rick told Priscilla as they climbed from his car.

Priscilla nodded, grateful to feel the ocean breeze on her face. She rarely became carsick. But the strain of seeing her mother again and putting up a false front had left Priscilla utterly drained.

She wished she could simply snap her fingers and the whole week would suddenly be over and everything back to normal. But the way she felt right now, Priscilla doubted she'd ever feel normal again.

"Oh, I wish Clara and Judy could see me now," Gloria exclaimed as she climbed the stairs behind her daughter. "It would just make them sick to think they're stuck up there in the woods while I'm down here on the beach."

"That's not a very kind thought, Mother."

"Well," Gloria began defensively. "You know how smug they both are about their sons. Clayton is a doctor now and from what Clara says he's raking in thousands. Course, you know how much stock you can put into what Clara says. For all we know, he's probably barely skimping by. And Judy's son, George, went into the military. She acts as though it was a grand patriotic gesture on his part. Hmmph! That kid never had a patriotic thought in his life."

"Mother, people do go into the military for an endless number of reasons," Priscilla patiently pointed out.

"Yes, I know. But there's no sense in Judy acting so haughty about it all. And you wouldn't be feeling so kindhearted, if you've heard some of the remarks they'd made about you."

Priscilla unlocked the door to her apartment and allowed her mother to proceed her through it.

"Probably that I was a boring schoolteacher," Priscilla said wearily.

"That's only one of the things," Gloria said, tossing her purse onto the chintz couch.

"It's pretty easy to guess one more," Priscilla replied. "Everybody back in Jefferson expects me to be an old maid."

Priscilla kicked off her heels and placed her purse on an end table. Behind her Gloria let out a trill of laughter.

"Well, you're going to show them all, aren't you darling? When they get an eyeful of Rick, that will shut them up."

With her back still to her mother, Priscilla closed her eyes and prayed for strength.

"I'm hardly marrying Rick for the sake of appearances," she muttered.

Suddenly her mother's hand was on her shoulder. "Of course you're not, darling," Gloria said gently. "And if I thought you were, I would be the first one to tell you not to." She turned Priscilla around to face her. "Darling, don't you know why I'm so happy about this engagement?"

Priscilla could guess, but at the moment she didn't want to go into it, so she merely shook her head.

Gloria reached up and stroked her daughter's

cheek. "It's because I love you, and because I've always known you deserved the best."

A lump of emotion filled Priscilla's throat and she blinked at the sting in her eyes.

"And there's really only one thing I need to know about this whole thing," Gloria went on.

"What—what is that?" Priscilla asked, her husky voice a little wary.

Gloria smiled, as though she knew the answer to her question even before she asked it. "Do you love Rick?"

Priscilla glanced toward the door as she heard Rick's approaching footsteps. It was a familiar sound, a sound that she had often listened for on those nights she'd felt lonely or down. The sound of Rick coming home had always lifted her heart, the sight of him had always made everything around her look wonderful. Why was she just now realizing that?

"Yes, I love him very much," Priscilla answered. Then wondered at the sudden relief she felt at just saying the words. She couldn't love Rick, could she? Not as she would a real lover, a real fiancé.

"Yes, it's obvious you do," Gloria said, "And I don't have to ask if he feels the same way about you. I can see it all over his face every time he looks at you."

The next moment Rick came through the door.

He took one look at Priscilla's pale face and asked, "Is anything wrong, Pris? I hope your mother hasn't given you a bit of bad news from home."

Shaking her head, Priscilla stepped away from her mother and went to take the cases from him. "It's—nothing is wrong. We were just having a little mother-daughter talk."

Gloria smiled indulgently at the two of them. "Actually I was just telling Priscilla that it was obvious how much you loved her. It's all over your face every time you look at her."

Was it? Rick had been practicing his look, but he didn't know he'd gotten his act down so well. What act? a voice inside him asked. You know you love Priscilla. Of course I love Priscilla, he told the voice. I've always loved her as a friend. But he didn't love her as a real lover, a real fiancée. Did he?

"That's what all my friends tell me, too," he told Gloria. "Yes, your daughter has really changed me."

That was probably the understatement of the year, Priscilla thought dryly. "I'll put these in the bedroom," she said. "Why don't you take Mother into the kitchen, honey, and I'll be there in just a minute."

He grinned at the honey. Priscilla never honeyed anyone past the age of ten. "We'll be waiting," he assured her, already taking Gloria by the arm.

In the bedroom, Priscilla tossed her mother's cases onto the bed and turned toward her dressing table. Her brown hair was windblown and the pink lipstick she'd started out with had long disappeared. The coral jersey dress she wore was belted tightly at the waist, making the full line of her breast obvious. Rick probably thought she looked fat in it, but it was the third one she'd tried on and she'd run out of time before they'd had to leave for the airport.

What am I doing? she asked the image in the mirror. She was in the process of deceiving her mother about something as sacred as an engagement, and now she was worrying that Rick might think she looked fat. You're losing it, Priscilla. Rick is not the concern here. It's your mother, and the fact that she truly believes you're headed toward marriage and babies.

With that grim reminder, she left the room and headed toward the kitchen.

While Priscilla prepared piña coladas, Rick carried plates and a tray of finger sandwiches out onto the deck.

"If you'd like to change out of your traveling suit," she suggested to her mother who was standing idly by, "why don't you go do it now, while Rick and I finish getting things together."

"It is rather warm outside," Gloria agreed.

"And slacks would be more comfortable. I think I will."

She left the room and Priscilla went about getting the rest of the snack ready. Rick came in from outside and darted a quick glance around the room.

"Where's your mother?" he asked.

Priscilla motioned with her head toward the other rooms. "Changing clothes."

He quickly went over to Priscilla and took her by the shoulders. "Are you okay?" he whispered.

She looked up at him, wondering why he was even asking. "Yes, I guess so. I just—oh, Rick, I hate deceiving my mother," she whispered back.

"Darling, don't think of it that way. You can see how happy you've made her already. That makes it worthwhile, doesn't it?"

She let out a long breath and continued in a low voice. "You don't have to call me darling. Mother isn't around."

He frowned at her, and growled beneath his breath, "Why are you biting my head off? I've always called you darling."

Priscilla was suddenly ashamed of herself. What he said was true. Only now it seemed different when he called her darling. Or was she only wanting to read something different into it? "Oh, I'm sorry, Rick," she said, resting her palms against the middle of his chest. "I'm so nervous, and I— I just don't know if I can keep this up. I never realized how awful it is to deceive someone you love.''

Rick took one of her hands and lifted it to his mouth. "Don't worry so, Pris. We'll get through this together. Now come on, chin up.''

Her skin burned where his lips had brushed it. She tried not to think of it as she lifted her face obediently up to him. "How's this? Do I look convincing?''

So convincing that Rick felt a heat rise up in him. "Perfect,'' he murmured. "So perfect I think I'll kiss you.''

"Rick—'' she started to protest, but before she could utter a sound, his mouth had already swooped down and covered hers.

Instantly her hands latched onto him and just as quickly her knees began to shake. Didn't he know what he was doing to her? she wondered wildly.

"I can see I'm not going to be able to leave you two alone for very long,'' Gloria teased, when she stepped back into the kitchen and found her daughter in Rick's arms.

Rick didn't hurry about ending the kiss. After all, he wanted to be convincing in this role as lover. Finally he lifted his head and chuckled softly down at Priscilla's bemused expression. "Priscilla gets carried away at times, Gloria.''

Priscilla bristled.

"I'm so glad to hear it," Gloria said.

Priscilla stared at her mother. "Mother, when I was still at home you would have died if a man had said that about me!"

Gloria laughed. "Priscilla, that was when you were young and inexperienced. I wanted you to be careful. But now you're a grown woman and Rick is going to be your husband."

Priscilla glanced up at Rick while resisting the urge to wet her still-hot lips. She wanted to be angry with him for the kiss, but found she couldn't be. "Yes, well Rick is a romantic. And he's—uh—taught me a few things about candlelight and poetry."

Gloria looked curiously at Rick. "You like poetry, Rick?"

Rick glanced pointedly at Priscilla before replying. "Yeats. There's nothing like a quiet evening with Yeats."

Priscilla nearly choked on his words. "Honey, please show Mother out to the deck and I'll bring the drinks," she suggested quickly.

"I'll be glad to," he said sweetly, leaning down and nuzzling Priscilla's cheek before turning to Gloria.

As the door shut behind the two of them, Priscilla discovered she'd been holding her breath. Air rushed out of her like a deflated balloon.

Behind her on the cabinet was a tray holding the

piña coladas. Impulsively she reached for the rum bottle and added a generous amount to one of the tall glasses.

Maybe the extra alcohol would fuzz her mind until she didn't care what her mother and Rick did or said, she thought hopefully.

But then it might not be good if she got too fuzzy, she rationalized. She might let something slip and give the whole thing away. No, she'd better give the one with the extra alcohol to Rick, she decided.

But what in heaven's name would he spout off if he got fuzzy, she wondered, still clutching the rum bottle. It would be her luck that he'd start talking about one of his girlfriends.

No, she'd better give the strongest drink to her mother. If Gloria got fuzzy she'd probably just rattle on about Tracie and her endless virtues.

On second thought, Priscilla could handle anything but that.

Oh, what the heck, she thought recklessly, quickly pouring a hefty shot of rum into the other two glasses. They could all get fuzzy, together, then none of it would matter. Hopefully.

Chapter Seven

The next morning after breakfast, Gloria began to dial Tracie's number in Dallas.

Priscilla, still wrapped in her bathrobe, was curled up in a wicker chair with a cup of coffee. "Mother, you tried to call Tracie all last evening. She'll probably be gone for the whole weekend."

Gloria shook her head and continued to push the buttons on the white telephone. "I won't be satisfied until I can get her."

Over the rim of her coffee cup, Priscilla watched her mother fidget nervously as she waited for her other daughter to answer the ring. Priscilla was secretly hoping Tracie wouldn't answer. As of now she was so angry with her sister that given the chance she didn't know what she might say to her.

"Tracie! Thank goodness you're finally home. I've been trying to get you since yesterday," Gloria said suddenly into the phone.

Priscilla swung her legs to the floor, and placed her coffee cup on a nearby table. If she was lucky, she could exit the room before her mother ever realized it.

"No, I'm not in Jefferson. I'm here at Priscilla's beach house. Yes, in Galveston. Tracie, you simply must reschedule your work load for the coming week."

Priscilla was halfway out of the chair when her mother's statement had her flopping back down on the cushion. She couldn't leave now, until she found out what her mother was up to.

"That's what I said. I want you to come to Galveston. Yes, I'm going to give Priscilla and Rick an engagement party, and naturally we want you here."

Priscilla gaped at her mother's back. A party? She hadn't mentioned anything about a party last night!

"Who is Rick? You know he's Priscilla's fiancé. How could you be so blank this morning, Tracie?" Gloria asked. "Were you out drinking last night? You know how I've warned you about alcohol ruining your skin."

Apparently Tracie began to respond, because

Gloria sat down on the edge of the couch and twirled the phone line with her free hand.

"Yes, I came down yesterday. Rick and Priscilla met me at the airport. It's been beautiful down here. And Rick is simply wonderful. You won't believe how handsome he is." She paused and a smug smile spread across her face. "Yes, he's simply a dream. Priscilla? Well, she's in love. How did you expect her to be?"

Priscilla wanted to groan and hold her head in her hands. Instead, all she could do was stare at her mother and wonder what her reaction would be if she suddenly told her the truth. Yet the image of her mother's tearful disappointment was enough to make her quickly discard the idea.

"I thought I'd see about a banquet hall in one of the local hotels for the party," Gloria continued. "What? Yes, I know it will be expensive, but that doesn't matter now. This is an important time in your sister's life. No, your father is on a fishing trip, so he won't be here—but he'll make up for it at the wedding and the reception, I assure you."

Gloria listened to her daughter a few more moments then handed the phone out to Priscilla. "She wants to speak with you."

Priscilla glanced from her mother to the phone, while torn between wanting to jump up and run out the door and yanking the phone from her mother to scream into the receiver.

Thankfully she was able to push aside both urges and speak evenly into the telephone. "Hello, Tracie. You wanted to speak to me?"

There was a pregnant silence, then Tracie suddenly whispered loudly. "What is going on down there, Priscilla? We both know you're no more engaged than I am! Who is this Rick Mother keeps raving about?"

Knowing her mother was watching her closely, Priscilla plastered a sweet smile on her face. "That's right, he is a dream. But of course I would say that."

"Priscilla, I know you're probably angry at me for dropping that little white lie on Mom, but—"

"That wouldn't begin to describe how I feel about it," Priscilla said cheerfully.

"I don't know what your game is, Pris, but we both know that when I talked to you the other day you insisted you hadn't even been dating a man."

Priscilla glanced away from her mother and out the window. Rick was on the deck, feeding bread to the gulls. The beautiful white birds screeched and hovered around his head while waiting for him to hold up a crumb.

"I'm afraid I neglected to tell you the truth about that. You see, Rick and I weren't ready to announce our plans before last week."

"Put Mother back on the phone!" Tracie virtually shouted in her ear. "I can see I'm getting nowhere with you."

Gloria took the phone again. "Are you coming, darling? At least by Wednesday. I'd like to have the party Friday night. What was that? Priscilla's ring? Oh, Tracie, it's simply fabulous. No, you don't need a microscope to see it. Believe me, you can see this one all the way across the room."

Gloria was suddenly all smiles. "You *are* coming. That's wonderful! Priscilla and I will be anxious to see you. Yes, we'll meet you at the airport in Houston. Maybe we can visit some bridal shops while we're there."

Oh, God, Priscilla silently groaned. This was getting too far out of hand. What was she going to do? And what was Rick going to think about all this? She glanced outside and saw he was still feeding the birds.

Quickly, while her mother was still talking to Tracie, she slipped out the door.

Rick grinned as he saw Priscilla stepping out the door, struggling to keep the rose-printed material of her robe wrapped around her legs as the ocean breeze tugged at it.

"Good morning, Pris, darling. Sleep well? If you made yourself another one of those piña coladas like we had yesterday it probably knocked you out completely."

Ignoring his comment, Priscilla hurried over to

him, glancing warily over her shoulder as she went. "Rick, you're not going to believe what is happening!"

His blue eyes narrowed on her face as he forgot the hungry sea gulls. "What? You didn't tell your mother the truth, did you?"

"No. But I'm beginning to think I should."

For a split second he'd imagined their engagement was over. It was a relief to discover it wasn't, though he couldn't imagine why. It wasn't Rick Lowrimore's style to be engaged. But being engaged to Priscilla was different, he quickly reassured himself. "Why? Is your mother still firing questions at you?"

Priscilla glanced again at the door, as if she expected her mother to walk through it any minute. "No, she's on the phone to Tracie. My sister is flying down here this week! And mother is planning to give us a party!"

"A party?" he repeated blankly.

"Yes! An engagement party! Oh, Rick, what are we going to do?" she groaned.

He looked thoughtfully out at the ocean, then back to Priscilla's dismal expression. "I can't see that we can do anything right now. Except try to put her off. I can always tell her that I can't get off work to go to Jefferson."

"Rick," she said wearily. "Mother is going to

give the party here at one of the hotels. This week. Friday, to be exact.''

''Oh, Lord,'' he muttered.

''Oh, Lord, is right. Rick, this whole thing is getting out of hand.''

''I admit I wasn't expecting this, but short of telling your mother the truth, I don't see anything we can do about it,'' he said.

Priscilla began pacing around the deck. ''When Tracie gets here I think I'll get her off to herself and strangle her!''

''Did you speak with her?''

Forgetting her robe, Priscilla leaned against the banister of the deck, grasping the top rail with both hands. ''Yes. But mother was right beside me. I could hardly say a thing. Anyway, I led Tracie to believe that we are truly engaged. Whether she believes it or not remains to be seen.''

Rick's eyes were instinctively drawn downward to where the wind was whipping Priscilla's robe away from her legs, revealing a tantalizing view of thigh. They were brown and soft and curvy. And they were making Rick's common sense go haywire. More than anything he'd like to reach over and glide his hands up those soft legs and...

''Rick! Are you listening to me? I said I told Tracie we're really engaged. It seemed like the only thing I could do.''

''Uh—yeah, I'm glad you told her. It's best that

only you and I know the truth about this," Rick said, while mentally trying to shake away thoughts of making love to Priscilla.

Yeah, she thought soberly. The truth was that the ring on her finger was a fake, and that the man standing beside her wasn't her fiancé but a pretender. If her Mother knew the truth, she'd be as disappointed in Priscilla as she'd always been with her in the past. And Tracie. Well, Priscilla was certain her sister would be smug about the whole thing.

Rick watched a defeated expression take hold of Priscilla's face and was suddenly reminded that he was going through this whole farce to help her. He didn't like seeing her upset, and wished there was something he could do to make things better for her. His own feelings would have to be sorted out later. "Priscilla, don't worry. We'll pull it off. If we have to, we'll go along with the party. After all, how hard is it to dance and eat?"

She looked up at him, a dry lift to her brow. "In front of our friends?"

For a response, he grinned devilishly and moved closer. "We have this thing down, Pris."

Curling his arm around her shoulders, he drew her next to his side. His hard body was warm, and the spicy scent of men's soap clung to his skin. Priscilla told her senses not to register the feel or scent of him. She told herself to ignore the urge to simply melt into him.

"I think we can fool anybody," he added.

She looked up at him and found her face only inches from his. There was a warm tenderness in his eyes that seemed so genuine Priscilla felt fooled herself.

But that look wasn't real, she quickly tried to tell herself. He'd just perfected an act to make everyone think he loved her.

"There you two are!" Gloria exclaimed. Priscilla looked around to see her mother hurrying toward them.

"Tracie kept talking and I couldn't get away," she continued on in a rush. "But rest assured, Priscilla, your sister will be here Wednesday. Isn't that wonderful news?"

"Wonderful," Priscilla repeated, forcing a smile on her face.

"Sisters should be together at a time like this," Gloria said matter-of-factly. "Don't you think so, Rick?"

"If they're close," he answered tactfully, his fingers absently kneading Priscilla's shoulder.

Gloria took a seat in one of the lawn chairs scattered across the deck. "Oh, they are close, Rick. There's only three years between their ages."

That was the only thing close about them, Priscilla thought. Tracie had never bothered spending time or sharing confidences with her younger sister. At school, Tracie had avoided Priscilla like the plague. It wasn't cool to have a younger sister who didn't run with the in crowd. So Priscilla had stuck to her books and her studies and watched from afar as Tracie flirted and charmed her way into any activity that would put her in the spotlight. Frankly, Priscilla figured the only reason Tracie was coming to Galveston now was to see Rick for herself.

She glanced up at him and for a moment his eyes caught hers before he turned his attention to Gloria. "From what Priscilla's told me, she and Tracie are nothing alike."

Gloria nodded. "That's true. But make no mistake, she can't wait to get here and help with the engagement party. Did you tell Rick about it, Pris?"

Priscilla nodded, hoping she didn't look as glum as she felt. "Mother, don't you think it's rather soon to be giving us a party? We've only just now told our friends about us."

"Nonsense! What reason is there to wait? I'm here. What could be a better time?"

"I can see your point," Rick said, "but it's not really necessary, and the cost of a party is so much these days."

Gloria patted her short hair, making sure the lacquered-down strands hadn't been moved by the wind. "No cost is too great, believe me," she said, smiling reassuringly at Rick. "I've waited for a long time to see my daughters married, and I want to enjoy every second of it."

Beneath his arm, Rick could feel Priscilla heave out a long breath. "I never realized this would make you so happy," she said to her mother.

Gloria's smile was glowing. "You girls came along late in my life. I didn't want it that way, but that's the way it happened. And now that your father and I have grown older, I was so afraid we'd miss out on the joys of grandchildren. But now I know that isn't going to be the case, it makes me happier than I can begin to tell you."

Priscilla wished she hadn't asked. Her mother's obvious joy made the whole deception seem that much worse.

"What about your parents, Rick?" Gloria asked. "Are they as happy as my husband and I are about your upcoming marriage?"

Rick hadn't even thought of his father these past few days. Since his mother had passed away, the two of them had seen less and less of each other. Yet he knew that if he were to ask his father's opinion on marriage, the old man would tell him to avoid it at all cost. "I'm sorry to say I lost my mother last year. But I can assure you that my father will be—very pleased."

Gloria's brows arched upward. "Will be? You haven't told him yet?"

Rick suddenly realized how strange that probably sounded and frantically searched his mind for a feasible excuse. "Er—no. He's been—overseas on an extended vacation."

"I trust he'll be here for the wedding," Gloria replied, rising to her feet.

"Mother! We haven't even set a date yet. You're getting way ahead of yourself," Priscilla swiftly interjected.

Gloria's grin was coy as she took in the sight of her daughter tucked closely in the crook of Rick's arm. "Somehow I don't think so. Now if you two will excuse me, I think I'll go get dressed."

After Gloria disappeared into the house, Priscilla looked wearily up at Rick. "She's hopeless. I guess you can see that for yourself."

He gave her shoulder a little squeeze. "I can see we're going to have our hands full this week. And I can see something else, sugar."

"What's that?"

His mouth twisted mockingly. "That you've made your mother one happy woman."

"Yes, I know." The knowledge should have had Priscilla feeling as if she were on top of the world. But the truth was, she'd never felt more miserable in her whole life.

Wednesday came all too quickly for Priscilla. After she and her mother had picked up Tracie at the airport, the three of them spent the entire afternoon going from one bridal shop to the next.

Tracie and her mother had insisted Priscilla try on at least half of all the dresses in each store. She'd had to come up with some kind of excuse as to why she didn't like any of the at least fifty she'd tried on. By the time they'd returned to the beach house Priscilla was totally exhausted. However, Gloria and Tracie were still going as strong as ever.

"Priscilla, Tracie's fixing coffee. Are you almost finished in there?"

Her mother's voice reverberated through the bathroom door. Priscilla pressed a cold, wet washcloth to her forehead before answering. "Yes, I'll be out shortly. Just give me a couple more minutes."

"Okay, darling," Gloria said, then followed it with, "Oh, there's the phone. Want me to get it?"

"Please," Priscilla said, hoping it wasn't anyone wanting to speak with her. At this moment, she was sure if she heard one more congratulation or one more question about the wedding her skull would simply crack down the middle.

"Priscilla," Gloria called. "It's for you, dear. And you might want to hurry. It's Rick."

Quickly tossing aside the washcloth, Priscilla rushed out of the bathroom and straight toward the phone. It would be just like Tracie to pick up the phone and pretend to be her sister.

"My, my," Tracie drawled as Priscilla flew by her in the hallway. "You must be crazy about this guy, or be trying to break your neck."

Priscilla ignored her sister and snatched up the receiver. "Yes, Rick."

"Hi, Pris. I just wanted to see if everything was okay. Did you pick up your sister at the airport? I've been trying to get you for the past three hours."

"We've just now gotten home," she explained. "We've been out shopping for a wedding gown."

"You're kidding."

"I'm afraid not," she answered, glancing back over her shoulder to see if Tracie was around. She was unsurprised to find that her sister had entered the room and taken up a relaxed position on the couch. "I didn't see a thing I thought you'd like— except the frilly garter belts, of course," she added with a soft, intimate laugh.

Rick bolted upright in his desk chair and stared quizzically at the receiver in his hand. "Priscilla? Have you been making piña coladas again?"

Priscilla laughed again, making it purposely husky. "No. But don't worry, Rick, darling. I'll find something especially sexy for our wedding night."

"You will? I'm finding this very interesting,

Priscilla,'' he said dryly, as he suddenly realized Priscilla was acting.

"Yes, I thought you would. But red is such a scandalous color for a honeymoon, darling. Still, I might consider it—just to please you,'' she purred into the receiver.

Across the room Tracie made a sickened noise. On the other end of the line, Rick said, "I take it you have company. Your sister?"

"However do you manage to know these things, Rick?"

"Just naturally brilliant, Pris, darling. But forget your sister. I want to hear more about red negligees,'' he teased. But he found he was imagining Priscilla's womanly curves hidden beneath a swathe of red lace.

"I'm sure you would. But I know you're busy there at work. Was there something special you wanted to tell me, honey?"

It always made him smile when Priscilla called him honey. He was smiling now, as his secretary entered his office. "Yes, there was, sweetheart. I wanted to let you know that I've made plans to take you and your mother and sister out to dinner tonight, so put on something pretty. And red would be sexy, Pris,'' he tacked on.

"Dinner? Are you sure?" She couldn't imagine Rick taking on such a trying situation.

"Of course, I'm sure. I want your sister to get

a good image of me.'' He wanted to make damn sure Priscilla's relatives knew how much he loved her. Or pretended to love her.

With her back carefully turned to Tracie, Priscilla let out a long breath. ''Whatever you say—darling. When should we be ready?''

''I'll be home at the usual time. Just give me time to change, once I get there.''

''Whatever you say. Goodbye, love,'' she added for good effect.

The faint smile on Rick's face deepened. He hadn't realized just how much he was going to enjoy these endearments Priscilla was bestowing on him. ''Goodbye, sugar.''

He hung up the phone and looked up at his secretary, who was smiling knowingly down at him.

''My fiancée,'' he said, unaware of the pride in his voice. ''I'm taking her and her family out to dinner.''

Handing him his opened mail, the secretary said, ''This woman has made you very happy. I'm glad for you.''

Rick looked at her with mild surprise. ''How can you tell?''

''Well, it's said that brides glow. But frankly, Mr. Lowrimore, I've seen a glow on your face ever since that first day you announced to the office you were getting married.''

Shocked by the woman's observation, he

reached up and absently rubbed his jaw. He was glowing? No. Surely not. He wasn't that good an actor, was he? She was probably just seeing razor burn. He'd been meaning to get new blades for the past week.

Priscilla slowly hung up the phone and turned to face Tracie. "Rick is taking us out to dinner. And he says to dress nicely. I hope you brought something, Tracie," she added just for mischief.

Tracie looked indignant. "All my things are nice." She watched Priscilla take a seat in one of the wicker chairs sitting opposite the couch. "You know, I really underestimated you, Pris. I never dreamed you'd carry things this far. I'm surprised you didn't let mother buy one of those expensive bridal dresses today."

Behind Priscilla's smooth expression, anger boiled like an angry volcano. "I will let her, when I find the right one." She knew it was foolish to talk this way, but she'd be damned before she let Tracie walk all over her. She'd done it all her life, and Priscilla was more than tired of it. "But I want to make sure Rick will like it, too."

"Bah," Tracie scoffed. "Who is this Rick, anyway? Some teacher you paid to act as your fiancé?"

For a moment Priscilla simply studied her sister. Tracie was known for her flippancy, but she wasn't usually this catty. Priscilla didn't know if it was because Tracie thought her sister was lying to her. Or if Tracie was jealous because, for once in their lives, Priscilla was in the spotlight. Whatever the reason, she couldn't wait for Rick to get here. He could handle Tracie. Tracie was Rick's kind of woman. The kind that was constantly flitting in and out of his life.

"Sorry to disappoint you, sister. He's an executive in sales for an oil firm in Houston."

Tracie swiftly leaned forward. "This is enough, Pris. I want the truth. You and I both know you're not really engaged! You're doing this just to get on mother's good side."

Something reckless came over Priscilla, and she shoved her hand in front of Tracie's face. "This diamond should prove how real my engagement is! Why are you so sure it's a fake? Maybe I don't have loads of talent like you. Maybe I have brown hair instead of blond like yours. And maybe I'm short instead of tall and willowy. But you know something, Tracie. Rick doesn't care. He loves me just the way I am!"

For once Tracie was taken aback by the fire in Priscilla's eyes. She fell back against the couch with a thump and a gaping mouth. "Well! You don't have to get so heated up with me," she said. "If you believe you're engaged, then I guess I do, too."

Priscilla knew that was as close as she would get to an apology from Tracie. It wasn't much, but then she'd never expected much in the way of sisterly love from Tracie. "While we're at this, Tracie. I'd like to hear why you took it upon yourself to tell Mother I was engaged?"

Tracie drummed her fingers against the arm of the couch as her expression changed to a guarded one. "I told you on the phone! I had to get her off my back." She leaned closer to Priscilla and lowered her voice. "Has she already started in about you having babies?"

"Yes. But that doesn't give you the excuse to tell—"

"Pris, what did my little white lie hurt?" she asked with a toss of her long blond hair. "Especially now that it turned out to be true, right?"

Good Lord, how could she argue with that, Priscilla wondered, feeling more and more defeated by the minute. "But what if it hadn't been true?"

Tracie shrugged as though she'd never given that question a second thought. "I don't know. Besides, I didn't expect her to come hightailing it down here the minute she heard the news!"

Priscilla supposed it was a surprise for Tracie to see their mother giving her sister so much attention. Even though it was misguided attention, she thought glumly. If the truth was known, Tracie

would surely think Priscilla didn't deserve the love
and attention her mother was giving her.

The idea tortured Priscilla and she rose from the
chair and moved restlessly around the room. She
wasn't doing any of this for herself, she silently
argued. She was doing it because she loved her
mother. Because she was finally able to give her
mother what she asked of her. Was that so bad of
her?

"Priscilla, I asked whether this Rick of yours
wants children?"

Tracie's too-sweet voice broke into Priscilla's
reverie and she paused to look at her sister. "Yes,
he does. Two, at least," she said, feeling her spirits
sink even lower.

Moving over to the windows, Priscilla looked
out at the ocean. Clouds were moving in from the
gulf, heavy gray-bottomed clouds that predicted
the night would bring rain. Priscilla wished she had
some sort of barometer that would predict the future the way a newsman predicted the weather. But
on second thought, knowing the future might be
painful. At least for now she and Rick were together. It wouldn't always be like that. Once this
ordeal was over Rick would go back to dating his
girls and Priscilla would teach her children and in
her off time bury her head in a book.

Tracie rolled her eyes heavenward. "Good heavens, this Rick must be as conventional as you, Pris-

cilla. I suppose next you're going to tell me you're planning on getting a station wagon and a house with a two-car garage.''

"Actually, Pris and Rick are going to continue to live here for a time."

The two girls looked up to see their mother entering the room with a tray of coffee.

"They like it by the ocean," she continued, "and I can hardly blame them for that."

Tracie raised her brows but said nothing.

Actually grateful for her mother's interruption, Priscilla crossed the room and took one of the coffee mugs. "Rick was calling to say he was taking us all out to dinner tonight, Mother. Do you feel up to it?"

"Oh, how lovely. Of course I'm up to it." She straightened up from placing the tray on the coffee table and smiled tenderly at Priscilla. "I haven't felt this wonderful in years. You and Rick have given my life a complete rejuvenation." With a happy sigh, she curled her arm around Priscilla's shoulders. "Love, marriage and babies. It's what I've always wanted for both my daughters."

Behind them on the couch, Tracie yawned. Priscilla, on the other hand, had to blink fiercely to ward off a wall of tears.

Chapter Eight

Priscilla searched every inch of her closet for something in red and was almost ready to give up when a red piece of fabric flashed between a U of T sweatshirt and her raincoat.

Quickly she jerked the clothes aside and pulled down the red garment. Oh, it was that one, she suddenly remembered. It was a full skirt gathered into a tight waist, with a bodice that was scooped low in the front and cut in a scandalously low vee in the back. Priscilla had bought the dress on an impulse for a dance given for the teachers, but at the last minute had decided not to wear it. Dancing was a contact thing, and she hadn't wanted all that skin exposed to men she knew only by passing in the hallways. But tonight was different. Tonight she'd be with Rick.

Tracie came into the bedroom just as Priscilla was pulling the dress up onto her shoulders. Her sister was already dressed in a pink sheath that showed off her tall, slim figure to perfection. Without even looking in the mirror, Priscilla already felt dowdy in comparison.

"Would you fasten the back for me?" she asked Tracie.

Tracie complied, then eyed her younger sister critically. "Don't you think that's a little low-cut? I can't ever remember you wanting to show cleavage before."

Priscilla turned and looked in the mirror. Actually there was only a hint of cleavage showing and the dress looked far better than she'd hoped. The color made her skin glow and the cut-in waist gave her full curves an alluring image. It suddenly dawned on her that maybe Tracie was jealous of the way Priscilla looked in the red dress. But that was preposterous. Tracie was the pretty one. She always had been. Hadn't every boy she'd ever thought about chosen Tracie over herself?

"Well, you know what they say," Priscilla said, trying her best to be glib with Tracie instead of hurt by her, "if you've got it, flaunt it."

Behind her in the mirror Priscilla could see Tracie glance down at her own rather small bustline. Priscilla's eyes suddenly filled with mischief.

"If you're worried about your appearance, Tracie, perhaps you should consult a cosmetic surgeon. Altering one's body seems to be all the rage now.''

Tracie spluttered with outrage. ''I don't want big breasts! Whatever gave you that idea? Everyone knows men this day and age love women for their brains. Not their bodies.''

Priscilla shrugged nonchalantly, but inwardly she was smiling with glee. ''That's odd. I remember you always telling me men loved women for their looks. Especially after you won the Miss Marion County beauty contest. Remember?''

Tracie walked primly to the mirror and began to adjust a blond curl on her shoulder. ''Of course, I remember winning. It was such a pleasure to beat April Jackson. She was going with Tommy Ferguson at the time. Remember her?''

Priscilla remembered all right. April had been a pretty girl with a sweet personality.

''You stole Tommy away from her and it broke her heart,'' Priscilla said.

Tracie waved the air with a multi-ringed hand. ''I didn't steal him—he just so happened to prefer me. And everybody said we were a far better-matched couple. Tommy won all-state for his quarterbacking that year, and I was the beauty queen of Marion County. We deserved each other.''

''You certainly did,'' Priscilla muttered under her breath.

"What?"

"I said I wonder what ever happened to April?" Priscilla asked innocently.

Tracie stood back from the mirror and smoothed the pink fabric over her hips. "Oh, Mother says she's married now and has three children. All I can say is what a waste."

Priscilla frowned as she began to brush her hair. "Not all women want to live the swinging single life, Tracie."

"Not all women know how to swing," Tracie said knowingly.

She reached down and took the hairbrush from Priscilla. "Here, let me do something with your hair. It looks so plain."

Thirty minutes later, Priscilla sneaked to the bathroom and carefully locked the door behind her. She wasn't about to let Rick see her with the hairdo Tracie had given her. It was moussed and teased so high she looked like she'd just encountered a UFO.

Grabbing the hairbrush, Priscilla went to work at removing the heavy teasing Tracie had insisted would give her a glamorous look.

By the time she could hear Rick's shower cut off, she'd smoothed her brown bob back in place and carefully pinned one side away from her ear with a clasp studded with red stones.

When she rejoined her mother and sister in the living room, Rick was on the other side of the wall, whistling as he pushed up the knot of his tie and reached for his pocket change.

"Priscilla! What did you do to your hair?" Tracie gasped as soon as Priscilla entered the room. "All that work I put into it is gone—ruined!"

"I'm sorry, Tracie. That look just wasn't me," she apologized.

"You look lovely, Priscilla," Gloria put in, as she watched Priscilla stuff a hankie into a small beaded purse.

Her mother's compliment surprised Priscilla. Compliments from her mother had been given so rarely in the past, and never about her appearance.

"You didn't tell me that," Tracie said, turning a pout on her mother.

Gloria's calm expression didn't alter. "You know you look lovely, Tracie. You always do."

The jangle of a bell suddenly sounded in the room. For a moment Priscilla simply stared at the door. Rick never used the doorbell. But, then, he'd never called on her family as her intended before, either.

"Are you going to answer the door, Priscilla, or should I?" Tracie asked with annoyance.

Priscilla hurried to the door and opened it. Across the threshold Rick was dressed in light gray slacks and a gray patterned shirt. A white tie was knotted at the small collar. Above it, his face looked so dear and his grin so familiar that much of the anxiety rushed out of her.

"Pris, darling, you wore red after all!" he exclaimed, his eyes running down the length of her.

She felt herself blushing. "I wanted to please you," she said, unaware of just how much truth there was in the words.

Rick could certainly say she had. Priscilla looked beautiful! He couldn't understand why he hadn't noticed it months ago.

"You did, sugar. You look beautiful." He stepped into the house and leaned down to kiss her softly on the lips.

Priscilla's hands went to his shoulders even though she was acutely conscious of her mother and sister behind them on the couch. It might be an act on his part, but Priscilla couldn't ignore the tantalizing feel of Rick's lips against hers. She was certain he had some kind of magic power that turned her knees to putty whenever he kissed her.

Finally he released her, and she turned a dreamy smile on Tracie. "Tracie, this is Rick. Rick, this is my sister Tracie."

A stretch of silence began to grow as Tracie simply stared at the sexy, fashionable man beside her sister. "You—you're Rick?" she finally stuttered.

A charming smile creased his darkly tanned face as he walked over and reached down for Tracie's hand. "That's right. It's a pleasure to finally meet you, Tracie."

Still dazed, Tracie rose to her feet. "Uh, yes. It's a pleasure to meet you too, Rick." She suddenly laughed in a gushing way as her eyes roamed over Rick's face. "I just didn't expect—well, you just don't seem like Priscilla's type, at all."

"Oh?" He glanced back at Priscilla. "Did you hear that, honey? And here I thought we were like two peas in a pod."

"You and Priscilla," Tracie repeated blankly, "like two peas in a pod?"

Priscilla instinctively edged close to Rick's side. As if it were the most natural thing in the world, he put his arm around her waist and drew her near to him. "I can't imagine my life without her," he told Tracie, knowing that much was the truth.

Tracie looked at her sister as if to say well, well. To Rick she said, "It seems my sister has been a naughty girl, keeping you a secret down here all to herself. All along I've been thinking she was leading a quiet life."

Rick laughed as though he found Tracie's remark very amusing. Priscilla's expression said she found it sickening.

"Priscilla's not always what she seems to be. In fact, she always keeps me guessing."

It was obvious Rick's remark stupefied Tracie,

but he didn't give her the chance to make a comment.

Glancing quickly around at the three women, he said, ''I don't know about you ladies, but I'm starving. Are we ready to go?''

They all murmured their agreement and trooped down the stairs to Rick's car, where he seated Tracie and Gloria in the back, then firmly ensconced Priscilla by his side.

''Is this your first visit to Galveston Island?'' Rick asked Tracie as he drove them westward down Seawall Boulevard.

''I came down three years ago, when Priscilla first moved here. To give her advice about decorating her apartment. I'm an interior decorator, you know.''

''And you haven't been back since? That's a pity. You should see more of your sister, and Galveston Island is a beautiful place to visit. I know Priscilla would love to have you.''

How could he have the nerve to encourage Tracie to come for frequent visits? Priscilla wondered angrily. Without thinking, she gouged her finger into Rick's thigh and twisted it back and forth. In response Rick's leg jerked, making his foot slip off the gas pedal. The car lurched forward, then suddenly slowed to a crawl.

''Well, Priscilla hasn't been up to Dallas to see me in at least a year,'' Tracie said defensively, her attention so taken by Rick's broad shoulders she was oblivious to the car's change in speed.

In the front seat Rick swatted at Priscilla's hand.

"Is something wrong with the car, Rick? It feels as though we're running out of gas," Gloria spoke up

"Er—no, I've just been having a little trouble with the carburetor. I'm sure it will be fine once it gets hold of itself," he added with a threatening look at Priscilla.

Feeling she'd gotten her point over, Priscilla took pity on Rick's leg and folded her hands demurely in her lap. "You failed to mention that I haven't been invited to Dallas in the past year," she said to Tracie, with a glance back at her sister.

Tracie gave a little laugh and darted a nervous look at her mother.

"Is that true, Tracie?" Gloria wanted to know.

Tracie spluttered. "Of course not! Priscilla knows she doesn't have to have an invitation to see her own sister. My house is always open to her."

Priscilla knew that if she'd taken it upon herself to surprise her sister with a visit she would have found her sharing the house with a man. Not that Priscilla wanted to be judgmental about Tracie's personal life, she just didn't want to intrude where she wasn't wanted. Tracie liked men for company, not a dull, boring sister.

* * *

Rick took them to a supper club with a tropical atmosphere. After cocktails, they were served a delicious meal of shrimp and crab legs. Throughout it all, Tracie was intent upon monopolizing Rick's attention. Priscilla wasn't surprised by her sister's behavior. When a handsome man was around, Tracie always had to have the lead role.

But Priscilla had to give Rick his due. He wasn't falling under Tracie's spell. In fact, Priscilla got the feeling he was going out of his way to prove himself in love with her. His hand continually reached to touch her, his smile was more often turned to her than anyone else, and when the dessert course was over he promptly led Priscilla out onto the dance floor.

"Rick, we really didn't have to dance. I'm not that good at it, anyway," she argued as he pulled her into his arms.

"What's there to be good at? All we have to do is shuffle our feet a little, and you put your head on my shoulder and look dreamy-eyed. It's easy," he told her.

She sighed as she settled into his arms. "I'm always forgetting your past, Rick. You know all about this love stuff."

Priscilla was all wrong about that, Rick thought. He knew about dating, charming and cajoling, but he didn't know what the word meant. But he did know that when he was with Priscilla there was a warm, contented feeling inside of him. It was unexplainable, and even if he tried to tell Priscilla how he felt, she would probably just laugh. When it came to women, she didn't think he had a serious bone in his body.

"You think I'm such a playboy." He took her hand and squeezed it against his chest.

"No, I don't think you are, I know you are. But when this is all over with, I'm going to find you a good woman."

He was with a good woman now. Rick knew that. He also knew good women weren't for him. Good women were the kind you married.

"And I'm going to find me a good man," she continued bravely. She didn't want to think that she was with a good man. But she'd known, almost from the moment she'd met him, that Rick was a good man. Trouble was, Rick had yet to learn that about himself. He didn't think he deserved a good woman.

The small band was playing the blues, and Priscilla blamed her sudden urge to cry on the woeful sound of the saxophone. To hide her melancholy, she rested her cheek against his chest and closed her eyes.

Rick shoved the thought of Priscilla finding another man out of his mind and pulled her closer, relishing the feel of her full curves pressed against him. Beneath his splayed hand her back was bare, soft and deliciously warm. Acting was nowhere in his thoughts, as his fingers slid up to her shoulder blades then back down to the small of her back.

"How do you like the woman I'm with now?" he whispered in a low voice, edged with amusement.

His mouth was close to her ear. Priscilla felt shivers rush down her spine. His hand on her back urged her so close that her breasts were flattened against his broad chest. She'd never been this close to any man, and certainly not to Rick. She could feel his heart beating against hers, feel the texture of his fingers as they played upon her skin. The heat and strength of his body was magnetic, drawing her to him like some unforeseen force.

"I like her," she said, trying her best to sound light and unaffected, "because I know she won't hurt you."

Her response surprised Rick, and he leaned back in order to see her face. "Oh? How do you know you won't hurt me?"

Humor dimpled his cheeks, but there was a seriousness to his voice that Priscilla didn't miss.

"Rick!" Her smile was rather quizzical as her head fell back and she looked up at him. "I could never, ever do anything to hurt you. You know that. To hurt you would be like hurting myself."

His smile was faint, as he lifted his hand and

toyed with the silky curtain of hair brushing her throat. "Sometimes I think—"

He was suddenly aware that the music had stopped and most of the couples were leaving the dance floor. The two of them probably looked conspicuous, but what the heck, Rick thought. They were engaged, they were supposed to be oblivious to everything but each other.

"You think what, Rick?" she prodded, her brown eyes searching his face.

"That you're too good for your own good," he finally answered. It wasn't what he'd really been going to say. He'd started to tell her that sometimes he thought they knew each other too well. How could he begin to impress her, when she already knew all his faults?

"I'm not good at all, Rick," she said, the smile suddenly falling from her face. "The only way I can make my mother happy is pretend to be something I'm not."

His fingers abandoned her hair to trace a gentle path over her chin. "Darling, why do you have to underestimate yourself? You've always made me happy."

He saw her eyes widen ever so slightly. "Have I, Rick?" she asked.

A wry smile curled up the corners of his mouth. Priscilla's eyes were drawn to it and her own lips yearned impossibly to feel his kiss again. It was crazy of her, but she couldn't seem to stop herself. Without even trying, Rick made her want him.

"Of course you have. Why else have you been my friend from the first moment we met?"

A lopsided smile spread across her face as she contemplated his words. "You're just gullible, Rick," she tried to tease.

He laughed softly, then glanced out the corner of his eye to their table across the room. "Tracie's giving us a look that says we're making spectacles of ourselves," he remarked.

"Tracie thinks I am a spectacle," Priscilla muttered as the band broke into another number.

"But your mother is positively beaming," Rick added smugly, "so let's dance again and make her twice as happy."

Priscilla had to laugh. It was either that or cry. "So now do you think you'll be able to see this engagement through?"

He gave her a cocky smile as they began to move to the music. "Easy. Like a snap." He pulled her head back down on his shoulder. "I never knew it would be like this to be engaged."

Unconsciously her hand tightened on his shoulder. "It isn't. This is only pretend."

Now why did she have to go and say that and ruin everything, he wondered. "Don't you think it would be this pleasant if it were real?"

Priscilla squeezed her eyes shut, closing out the

dim lights and the couples circling slowly around them. "First of all, you wouldn't be dancing with me, because you wouldn't be engaged to me. And me—well, I wouldn't be dancing, because most of the men I know, the kind who would even contemplate getting themselves engaged to me, aren't dancers—like Williard, for instance. I can't see myself like this—with him. Even if we were engaged."

"Thank God!" Rick muttered.

"And if this engagement was real, I wouldn't be wearing a ring like this, or should I say one that looks like this," Priscilla went on.

Over her head, Rick's mouth tightened into a frustrated line. "You mean it would be real instead of fake."

"No. I mean it wouldn't be this expensive-looking. You're the only man I know who has to pay income tax instead of getting a refund back."

Rick laughed. "Sugar, that's not because I make a big salary. That's because I'm a bachelor."

Suddenly Priscilla giggled. "You might like to know that Tracie was goggle-eyed over the ring. Isn't that ridiculously funny? She thinks she has such good taste."

"Priscilla! You're talking about my taste. I picked out the ring, remember?"

She gave a little shrug. "Well, you know what

I mean, Rick. She didn't realize she was looking at a fake.''

"Do you have to keep using that word? It makes me feel cheap," he said tersely.

"This whole thing makes me feel cheap," Priscilla confessed. "Before Tracie met you, she accused you of being a fellow schoolteacher that I had to pay to pose as my fiancé."

He laughed, and she immediately pinched his shoulder. "How can you laugh, Rick? Do you know how much it hurts when she says things like that to me?"

His voice was suddenly contrite. "Why should it hurt? It's obvious Tracie is a spoiled, self-centered brat. It shouldn't matter what she says."

She looked up at him with shadowed eyes. "Maybe Tracie is all that, but she's still telling the truth. The only kind of fiancé I could get is a pretend one."

As Rick looked down at her, he suddenly wanted to shake her. He wanted to tell her that holding her in his arms was the most real, the most right thing he'd ever known. He wanted to tell her that she was a beautiful woman in her own right, and that she was worthy of a man's love. His love.

But he couldn't do any of that. He couldn't lay himself open like that. Love wasn't for him, and marriage was certainly off the books. The last thing on earth he'd want to do was marry Priscilla and

see her become listless and unhappy. The only
thing he remembered about his parent's marriage
was the fights. Either hot, violent ones, or cold,
accusing ones. To a young, impressionable boy,
home had seemed like a prison where anger and
resentment had boiled just beneath the surface. He
didn't want that for him and Priscilla. They were
happy now. Why should he ruin it all by marrying
her?

"Be quiet, Pris, darling," he said in a hushed
voice. "I don't want to hear any more about fakes,
lies or pretend. Let's just remember why we're doing this. And once your mother goes home, it will
all be over with."

Yes, it would all be over with, Priscilla silently
agreed. Rick would be free to go back to dating
his women, and she would be back to being in bed
by ten o'clock. Priscilla could hardly bear the
thought.

Over. Rick's mind dwelled on the word. He
didn't want it to be over. At least not entirely. But
that was his heart talking, not his head. And Rick
was a man who never listened to his heart.

That's because your heart has never spoken to
you before, you idiot, a frustrated voice reasoned
inside his head. Priscilla's the only woman your
heart could ever respond to.

The voice frightened Rick and he quickly
pushed it out of his head, blaming it on the dancing

and having Priscilla in his arms. He was a totally confirmed bachelor. And even if he wasn't, that didn't mean Priscilla wanted him in a serious way, he reasoned. Good heavens, she didn't trust him as far as she could throw him.

Priscilla stirred in his arms. Rick pulled his thoughts back to the present and looked down at her. Her face was lifted up and her brown eyes were misty as they connected with his.

"This is so nice, Rick. Thank you for bringing me out tonight—and the dancing. I can see why you go out so much now. And you know what?"

"No. What?" he asked, totally bemused by her.

"When this is all over, I'm never going back to living the dull life."

Her words shocked him back to reality. "Priscilla—"

"No, Rick. Don't try to dissuade me. For the past year you've been telling me I need to loosen up, go out, enjoy myself. Now I can see you were right. You've shown me what I've been missing by burying myself in my job and my books."

"Priscilla, I didn't really mean—"

"To be honest," Priscilla interrupted, her expression suddenly serious, "I've always been afraid of dating. Or at least dating anyone I could really like."

Rick frowned. "Well, I can't imagine why you

would want to date someone you couldn't like,'' he said dryly.

''So I wouldn't have to worry about losing them,'' she quipped.

He looked at her as if she'd taken leave of her senses.

Priscilla released a weary breath. ''Look, Rick, up until I graduated from high school and left home, I always had to compete with Tracie. And I'm sure I don't have to tell you I always came up with the short end of the stick when it came to men. They would take one look at Tracie and forget about me.'' She shook her head, her expression grim. ''I made the mistake of falling for a boy in my senior year. But I thought he was sincere and truly different from all the other boys who considered brain power low on their list of date qualifications.''

''He wasn't different?'' Rick asked, already hating this unknown teenager for hurting his Priscilla.

She shook her head. ''He was only using me as a stepping-stone to get to Tracie. I found this out one evening when I came down the stairs expecting to find him waiting to pick me up for our date. Instead, I found him kissing Tracie.''

''Poor Pris. You should have gone at both of them with a baseball bat.''

''I wanted to. But then my common sense told me that neither one of them was really worth it.

Tracie ended up dating him twice and dropping him.''

"At least he got his due," Rick said with malicious glee. "But what about Tracie?''

Priscilla sighed defeatedly. "Well, I've always had to overlook Tracie. She has a weakness for the opposite sex. Sorta like you, Rick.''

"Thanks, Priscilla,'' he said tersely.

Ignoring his sarcasm, Priscilla went on in a brighter tone. "Still, I don't think I ever quite got over it—until now,'' she added. "Now I see I can't go around all my life expecting all men to be like Bobby Joe McCulla. I've got to be positive, from now on. If I get out there and get my heart broken, I'll just have to get over it and try again. Besides, it might be fun playing the field. You certainly seem to enjoy it.''

Why did it seem the tables were turning on him. This was not the way he wanted Priscilla to talk! "Priscilla, you can't expect—"

"I know. I know. I'll probably have trouble finding men of quality to ask me out. But I've been thinking about that, too, Rick. I've decided to go to one of those places where they make you over. You know, hair, body, makeup. I can lose ten or fifteen pounds and get that scrawny look, a perm in my hair and the right kind of makeup on my face. Maybe I could even take one of those how-to-succeed courses.''

Rick looked horrified. He didn't want Priscilla to change. Not one inch of her! "Priscilla, this is insane. You are—"

"The song is over, Rick," she quickly interrupted, while glancing around his shoulder to see most of the couples leaving the dance floor. We'd really better go back to the table now."

Rick wanted to argue, but decided this wasn't the time or place. He'd wait and get her out on the beach where he could give her a good yelling at.

Changing her looks! Playing the field! She was out of her mind, if she thought he was going to stand by and let her do such things.

"I really think we'd better be getting back home," he said, as they walked off the dance floor. He was eager to get her alone, and put her mind back on its proper track. "This place has done something to your head, Pris."

She squeezed his hand and tossed him a smile. "Not the place, Rick. You. You've made me see that living entirely alone is not the right course for me."

Priscilla also knew that once this was over, she was desperately going to need someone to take her mind and her heart off Rick. But of course she couldn't tell him that.

It suddenly dawned on Priscilla that besides deceiving her mother and sister, she was now going to have to deceive Rick. It was going to kill her.

"I wondered if you two were ever going to get off the dance floor," Tracie said drolly, as Rick helped Priscilla back into her seat.

After taking his own seat, Rick smiled wickedly over at her. "When Priscilla and I are in each other's arms we forget about time. I hope you two weren't bored," he added, including Gloria in his glance.

"Of course we weren't, Rick," Gloria hastened to assure him. "It gladdens my heart to see my daughter dancing with the man she loves."

Priscilla looked down at her half-filled wineglass and fought the urge to burst into hopeless sobs.

Chapter Nine

Gloria and Tracie chattered continually throughout the ride back home. Priscilla remained quiet, staring thoughtfully out the window at the black, moonless night.

Tonight she'd realized that she was losing Rick. Not just as a pretend fiancé, but losing him altogether. Things would never go back to the way they used to be. How could they? Her feelings had changed for him. How could she be happy just being his friend? How could she be happy sitting on the sidelines while he resumed his life as a playboy?

Behind the wheel, Rick inserted noncommittal remarks to the conversation, but his attention was barely on what either Tracie or Gloria was saying.

His mind was really on Priscilla and the change he could see coming over her. He had to do something to stop it. But what? If she wanted to go out with other men, who was he to say she couldn't?

When the four of them reached the beach house and climbed out of the car, Rick quickly said to Tracie and Gloria, "If you two will kindly excuse us, I'd like to take Priscilla for a walk on the beach."

"Please do," Gloria said. "You two need some time alone."

As she and Tracie started up the stairs, Priscilla's desperate gaze followed her mother's back. She didn't want to be alone with Rick. It was becoming too painful. "Rick, I really am tired—"

"Come on, I want to talk to you," he said, quickly taking Priscilla by the arm.

"What do we possibly need to talk about tonight?" she muttered, as he led her away from the house and down onto the damp beach.

"You!"

"Me? We can talk about me anytime. I want to go to bed," she said with annoyance.

"You can go to bed when I get through with you," he said with just as much annoyance.

Priscilla jerked her elbow away from his grasp. It wasn't like Rick to be demanding. "Don't talk to me like—like you're my husband or something! Because you're not!"

Seeing they were getting off on the wrong track, Rick stopped walking and threw up his arms in surrender. "Okay, Priscilla. I'm sorry. I just wanted you to give me a minute. That's all," he said in a gentler voice.

Priscilla's head dropped. She was overreacting and he was probably wondering why. "I'm sorry, too, Rick. I guess the stress of this whole thing is getting to me." She looked up at him as she tried to see his face in the darkness. "What did you want to talk to me about? Have I done something wrong?"

He grimaced. "Not yet. But I'm beginning to wonder," he muttered.

Her face wrinkled with confusion. "What are you talking about? I haven't let anything slip about this whole deception."

Rick shook his head. "That's not what I mean, Pris. I'm talking about you and this tangent you seem hell-bent on taking. What's gotten into you, Priscilla?"

Priscilla suddenly looked away from him. "Nothing, Rick. Is it any crime to want to change yourself a little?"

"A little! My God, you're talking about a major make-over here. And it's totally unnecessary. You don't need to change anything about you."

Turning her back to him, she took a couple of steps toward the rolling swell of waves breaking on the beach. "I do, if I'm ever going to find a real husband."

Rick winced at her words. "What makes you think you need a husband?" he asked, his voice edged with frustration. He didn't know how to deal with the strange, unexpected reactions he was having toward Priscilla. And he especially didn't know how to deal with her.

She shrugged and he moved toward her. He couldn't stop himself from putting his hands on her shoulders, spreading his fingers so that they touched the soft skin of her back.

"Well, not necessarily a husband," she said in a small voice. "But at least—a male companion."

"A male companion," he echoed blankly. "What would you label me?"

At his question, she turned to face him. "A friend. You've always been a friend to me, Rick. But—but it's not the same. I need more." She sighed and shook her head as she searched for the right words. "You know what I mean, Rick. You've always had me for a friend, but that didn't stop you from dating other women."

How could he argue with that? he wondered sickly. "I—it's not that I don't want you to date, Priscilla. It's just that—" He stopped suddenly, as he realized he was lying and feeling horrible about it. He'd never lied to Priscilla in his whole life, until this engagement thing had started. "I don't want you to change. You're perfect just the way you are.''

Her features softened and she smiled up at him. ''That's the friend in you talking, Rick. But we both know if I'm ever going to attract a man, I'm going to have to be attractive.''

He lifted one hand to her face and cupped her cheek in his big palm. ''Darling, you are attractive. When are you going to realize that? The real reason you don't attract men is because you never go anywhere to attract them. And when you do, you always have a sign around your neck that says stay away.''

''No, I don't,'' she protested. His touch was making her giddy and the things he was saying, what did it all mean?

''You just told me yourself that you've always been afraid to date, afraid you'd get close to someone and then lose him,'' he reasoned.

''That's—that's true, I was. But that's because I never had much confidence in myself. If I change myself for the better, then I will have the confidence to—to become involved with a man.'' Priscilla felt like the biggest liar that ever walked the earth. She was already involved with a man, she thought miserably. Her heart was totally, completely involved with Rick. It amazed her that he couldn't see it.

Rick felt as if she were jabbing a knife in his

midsection, then turning the blade. He didn't want her to get involved with a man. Was he going to have to spell it out in black-and-white? Hell, yes, that voice said inside his head. She doesn't know you care about her.

He felt Priscilla reaching for his hand. With an eagerness all their own, his fingers entwined with hers.

"Rick, I know you're my friend and I know you're only showing your concern for my welfare. But believe me, you don't have to worry. I know a good man now from a Bobby Joe McCulla."

He doubted it, but what could he say? So many times in the past Priscilla had done this very same thing to him. Wasn't it just a few days ago she'd been trying to warn him off frivolous women? But the thing with him now wasn't women. It was woman. More specifically her. And to be honest, he was finding Priscilla much more dangerous than any of those fluffheads he'd dated in the past. He'd started this thing out because he'd wanted to protect Priscilla from her relatives. Now he was the one who needed protecting.

"I hope to God you do, Pris. I'd never want you to be hurt." Unconsciously, his hand on her face began to move. Before he knew it, his finger had strayed to her lips, touching them with an awed reverence. "I care about you. Surely you know that by now," he whispered.

He cared about her, yes. As a friend. The sting of tears touched her eyes, but she forced herself to smile brightly up at him.

"Yes, I know," she murmured. She pulled away from him and started back toward the house. After a few yards she glanced over her shoulder to see Rick was yet to move an inch. "We'd better go in, Rick, and get some rest," she urged. "Tomorrow night is the party, and God help us, I'm sure we're going to need all our strength to get through it."

The strong gulf wind was whipping her red dress against her body. All Rick could think about was the way she looked—her full breasts, small waist, the flare of her hips, and the way she felt to him whenever he touched her. In that moment he wished desperately that he could carry her to a secluded place on the beach and make endless love to her.

"Yeah. I guess we should," he said, his gaze turning toward the beach house. The lights on Priscilla's side of the duplex were blazing brightly, reminding him that he was playing out a role, a role that was becoming all too real for his guarded heart.

Priscilla was groggy-eyed when she stumbled into the kitchen the next morning and found Tracie and her mother sitting at the table eating toast and drinking coffee.

"Good morning, darling," Gloria said cheerfully. "I'm glad you're up. There's so much to be done today. The first of which is to find a dress for you to wear tonight. Do you think we should take a cab over to Houston?"

Priscilla silently groaned as she pulled a coffee cup down from the cabinet. She'd never felt so exhausted in her life. She'd spent the biggest part of the night awake, mulling this whole farce over and over in her mind. If something didn't happen soon she was going to lose her mind.

"Mother, Houston is almost fifty miles away. We'll find a dress here on the Island."

"You don't have to be so snappy," Tracie scolded. "After all, Mother is going out of her way to do all this for you."

Priscilla picked up the carafe from the coffee machine and poured her cup full. "I'm not being snappy," she said. "And if I sounded that way, it's simply because I didn't get enough sleep."

Frowning, Tracie broke off a tiny nibble of dry toast. "If Rick hadn't kept you out on the beach so long last night, you would have gotten plenty of sleep."

Priscilla didn't miss the jealous note in her sister's voice. If she hadn't felt so miserable, she would have laughed at the absurdity of it all. Tracie had never been jealous of any man Priscilla had managed to attract. But now that she had a pretend one, things were different.

"If you ever get engaged, Tracie, you'll understand why you need time alone with your fiancé," she quipped, unable to hide her annoyance at her sister. Her heart was aching. She was losing Rick. And Tracie was the one who had started it all with her thoughtless selfishness.

"That's right, Tracie," their mother put in. "You flit from one boyfriend to the next. You don't really know what it's like to have a true love such as Priscilla has."

Priscilla tried not to listen to her mother's words as she dropped two slices of bread into the toaster.

"I beg your pardon, Mother!" Tracie gasped. "I've been in love several times."

In love with herself, Priscilla thought wearily as she sipped the hot coffee and waited for the toaster to pop.

"I'm not stupid, Tracie," Gloria said, surprising both her daughters. "I might be old, but that doesn't mean I've forgotten what it's like to be in love."

"Of course you haven't forgotten," Tracie sniffed. "You're still in love with Daddy."

The older woman smiled patiently at her older daughter. "That's true. But when a person first falls in love, there's just something about the way they look, the way they behave. Thank God I can read it all over Priscilla. Unfortunately I've never seen it in you, Tracie.''

Tracie looked indignant. "Well, frankly I don't think a woman needs a husband or children to be happy. Why, more and more women are choosing careers over families. But, then, teaching school isn't really a career," she said, with a pointed look at Priscilla. "It's just a job. Whereas interior decorating is something with which I can expand and climb the ladder.''

The toaster popped and Priscilla quickly spread the toast with butter and honey. She didn't need the extra calories, but after spending the past three days in Tracie's company, she felt she deserved them.

"And climbing the ladder has always been important to you, hasn't it?" Priscilla asked as she carried her breakfast to the table and took a seat to the left of her mother.

Tracie rose from her chair and carefully brushed the crumbs from her fingers. "It's not a crime to be ambitious. You should try it. Rick would probably find it refreshing.''

The remark hurt, but Priscilla blamed herself. She should have never put herself in such an impossible situation in the first place.

"Rick loves me the way I am. I know that's hard for you to believe, but he does,'' Priscilla said.

"Now, girls, please let's not be tacky to each other this morning," Gloria put in quickly.

Seeing her mother was serious, Tracie suddenly laughed and hurried around the table to Priscilla to give her a cheeky hug. "Mother, don't be silly. You know Priscilla and I love each other. But we're sisters, it wouldn't be normal if we didn't argue. Right, Pris?"

It was impossible not to love Tracie, Priscilla thought. Even though she was smug and catty and spoiled. In a way, she couldn't be blamed, because their parents had always coddled her. And when everything else was put aside, she was her sister.

"We have always argued," Priscilla agreed. "Why should that change just because we're older?"

"You're so sweet." With great aplomb, Tracie kissed her sister's cheek then headed toward the door. "Now I'm off to the shower. You two hurry, so we can go shopping. I must find myself a dress, too."

Priscilla sighed, more out of relief than anything, as Tracie disappeared around the door.

Gloria sighed, too, but not for the same reason. "I'm worried about that girl."

Priscilla looked at her mother. "Worried? Why? Tracie is no different than she ever was."

Gloria shook her head as she sipped her coffee.

"Underneath all that bravado, I think she's terribly unhappy."

Priscilla couldn't imagine it. Tracie had always had everything and anything she wanted. "You can't be serious. Tracie loves her job." She looked a bit closer at her mother. "To be honest, I never thought you noticed that about Tracie."

Gloria's brows lifted in question.

"The bravado," Priscilla explained with as much tact as she could. "You've always been so proud of Tracie. Of her talents and beauty. I never thought you saw the other side of her."

Gloria smiled gently. "Naturally I've always been proud of Tracie. But that doesn't mean I'm blind to her faults. It doesn't mean I haven't always been proud of you, either," Gloria went on.

Priscilla couldn't believe her ears. "Proud of me?"

"Don't look so surprised, darling," she said with a laugh that was half-scolding. "You are my daughter, too, you know." Gloria got up from the table and went to pour herself another cup of coffee.

Priscilla's eyes followed her mother. "Yes—but—but I've never been like Tracie. I could never do the things she did."

With a confused frown on her face, Gloria looked back at her daughter. "Is that what you thought? That I wanted you to be like her?"

Priscilla had always thought so. Now she wasn't so sure. "I thought—I thought you always wanted me to be, well, prettier than I was—and more popular, like Tracie."

Gloria shook her head. "Darling, Pris, I've never wanted you to be like Tracie. If I pushed you to do things, it was because I wanted it for you."

Priscilla's expression said she couldn't quite believe what her mother was saying. Throwing her hand up in a frustrated gesture, Gloria came back to the table and took her seat.

"Pris, I know that these things have always come easily to Tracie. Perhaps too easily. And I know that in certain areas you've had to work harder than she. But that doesn't mean you're any less worthy."

A part of Priscilla's heart was filled with warmth and joy at hearing her mother's words, but the other part was aching, because all this time she'd been lying to her mother, whom she loved very much.

But if she told her mother the truth now, she silently reasoned with herself, her mother's heart would be crushed. If she hadn't had a low opinion of Priscilla in the past, it would certainly give her one now to find out her daughter was a liar.

Priscilla's gaze dropped to the tabletop. "When—when you first arrived here in Galveston, you couldn't believe I'd found someone like Rick,'' she murmured doubtfully.

Gloria looked at her daughter as though she was seeing her for the first time. ''Priscilla! That wasn't because I thought you were incapable—or unattractive. To be honest, I had it in the back of my mind that you'd totally deserted the idea of men and marriage. It was simply wonderful to find you with Rick.''

A gentle smile spread across her face as she reached over and patted Priscilla's arm. ''I know it must seem that I want this marriage for myself. But that's not so. I want it for you, darling, because I know sharing your life with Rick is going to make you very happy.''

Priscilla's throat was suddenly clogged with emotion. ''I—yes, Rick does make me happy. He's a wonderful man.'' It was so true, she thought. She was more certain of it now than she'd ever been.

Gloria gave her a final pat on the arm. ''That's enough serious talk. Hurry and finish your breakfast so we can go find a dress for you to wear tonight. You're going to knock everyone's eyes out at the party, especially Rick's.''

The party was to take place in a posh seaside hotel. Gloria had worked nonstop making the arrangements and contacting those people that Rick and Priscilla wanted to invite. Yet it wasn't until a couple of hours before the party, that the whole thing really came home to Priscilla.

She was shaking all over as she dressed and attempted to make up her face. To make matters worse, Rick was late getting home. Gloria and Tracie had already left to see to last-minute details and Priscilla was pacing through the empty house waiting to hear Rick's footsteps.

When he finally arrived home, Priscilla rushed through the door connecting their kitchens and out to his cluttered living room. "Rick, I thought you'd never get here! We're supposed to be at the party in thirty minutes!"

He was in the process of tossing his briefcase on a desk. He looked around at the sound of Priscilla and immediately did a double take. "Priscilla!" he said hoarsely, his eyes riveted on her. "What have you done to yourself?"

Her nervousness increased, as she glanced down at herself. Her dress was made of a silky fabric patterned with swirls of pink and turquoise, styled with a *bustier* bodice and a skirt that draped her hips with a swathe of fabric that knotted at her hip. She'd thought the dress was a bit daring, since it had no shoulders, but her mother and Tracie had insisted she looked good in it. Which, coming from Tracie, was quite a concession.

"I don't know. Is something wrong?" Priscilla asked worriedly.

"Wrong? Priscilla you look like an exquisite vision." He walked toward her, his eyes gleaming. "I've never seen you looking like this."

She rubbed her hands nervously down her hips. "I'd feel more like myself in a pair of shorts and a T-shirt," she admitted with a shaky laugh, not really knowing how to take his compliment.

He stopped just inches in front of her. Before Priscilla could guess his intentions, his hands came out to span her waist. "All my friends are going to be jealous as hell tonight when they see you," he murmured.

Her vague smile said she didn't quite believe him. "So are mine, when they get a look at you. They'll also think you're marrying me for my money."

He laughed. "Priscilla, you don't have any money."

"They'll think I do, after tonight."

He swatted her on the hip, then pushed her away from him. "Sit down and calm yourself while I shower. I'll be ready to go in just a few minutes."

Priscilla was too keyed up to sit down. After Rick disappeared, she moved around the room straightening objects and picking up dirty clothes and dishes.

Ten minutes later Rick came back into the room, a tie dangling from his forefinger. "Can you tie this for me, darling? I seem to be all thumbs this evening.''

He couldn't be nervous, too. Rick was never nervous. She took the tie from him, then gave him a hopeless look. "Rick, this is a bow tie. They're impossible to tie. Go find a clip on and let's get out of here. Everyone is going to be wondering where we are.''

"This is the one that goes with this jacket, Pris. Just try. Please. I want to look good for you tonight,'' he added, his eyes gleaming back at her.

"Oh, all right. But I want you to know I wouldn't do this for anyone else.'' She raised on tiptoe and slipped the strip of dotted material around his neck. The background of the tie was a pinkish-brown color that matched his jacket. The dots were a darker brown that matched his slacks. Only a man like Rick could get away with wearing such a color, especially with a bow tie.

"You smell wonderful, Priscilla. Is that the jasmine stuff you wore for Williard again?'' He sniffed at her hair while she fumbled with the tie.

"No, it is not. It's supposed to be exotic, like a tropical island,'' she said crossly. How could he mention Williard at a time like this?

Captivated by the scent, Rick sniffed again. He didn't have to close his eyes to imagine a secluded tropical island, Priscilla on the beach with nothing on but her butternut-brown skin. From out of nowhere, he'd come to her and she'd open her arms to him. A warm trade wind would caress their bodies with the balmy, sweet scent of flowers. Above their heads, colorful birds would wing from palm to palm, their discordant screeches and calls somehow harmonizing with the restless sound of the sea.

Priscilla's brown eyes would be dreamy, full of love, as he took her into his arms and lowered his mouth to hers. Her lips would be deliciously sweet, her breasts luscious and full against him....

"Rick! Did you hear me?" Priscilla nearly shouted.

Rick shook his head as her question invaded his erotic imaginings. "Uh—what were you saying? I'm afraid my mind was drifting," he said, unaware of the faint red blush creeping up his face.

"I'm sure," she said tersely. "Probably to your little black book. So you could decide who it is you'd really like to be tieing this tie."

Rick's eyes suddenly darted down to her face as he realized he hadn't thought about his little book, as Priscilla called it, in a long time. The only woman he could think about was Priscilla. The only woman he wanted was Priscilla. It amazed him that she hadn't figured that out. "Priscilla, why don't we—"

The words hung in his throat. My God, what was he doing, he asked himself. He'd been about to say

elope together! But he wasn't a man who wanted
to marry. Just because he could imagine a delicious
honeymoon on a tropical island, didn't mean hap-
pily-ever-after would follow.

"Why don't we what?" she asked blithely, still
straightening the ends of his tie.

His eyes glanced away from her and he swallowed hard, in an effort to get a hold on himself.
"Why don't we get going? Everyone will be wondering where we are."

Priscilla looked at him and hopelessly shook her
head. "I just told you that a few minutes ago,
Rick."

Had she? He was losing his mind. "Sorry, Pris.
My day has been very hectic." Actually he'd
thought about nothing but her and how this whole
thing might end.

"Oh? Did you negotiate a big deal today?" she
asked.

"Something like that," he said evasively, while
taking her elbow.

"Wait, Rick. My purse is back in the kitchen."

He reluctantly released her arm, and Priscilla
hurried out of the room as fast as her high heels
would allow. When she returned, he gave her a wry
smile.

"Ready to be thrown to the lions?"

She groaned. "Please, Rick, I already feel bad
enough as it is."

"Don't worry, you'll be fine." He opened the door and guided her through it.

"What about you?" she asked as they hurried down the steps. "Have you forgotten your in-love look?"

Rick nearly missed a step as he jerked his eyes over to her. Somewhere along the way his acting had ceased. Now when he looked at Priscilla with love it came as naturally as breathing. But he couldn't tell her that. She might get the crazy idea that he was in love with her for real. "Not hardly. Olivier doesn't have anything on me."

"Well, I was sort of fancying myself as a young Bette Davis. In fact, I've gotten so good at acting, my mother truly believes I'm madly in love with you."

Rick felt something sick turn inside of him as he helped Priscilla in the car. "You don't look anything like Bette Davis," he said, his voice unusually cross.

Priscilla's brows lifted as she watched him walk around the car then slide behind the wheel. "I do have brown eyes," she retorted. "Besides, I was talking about my acting. Don't you think I'm getting better?"

He tossed her a dry look as he backed the car out onto the street. "I think you should go into the theater instead of back to school next year."

Her expression was suddenly quizzical. "Are you angry with me for some reason?"

Rick sighed. No, he wasn't angry with her. He was angry at himself, for ever allowing his feelings for Priscilla to go so far. "No. I'm not angry. I'm just dreading the party, that's all."

Priscilla's head dropped. "I'm sorry, Rick."

His eyes were on the traffic as he negotiated the car onto a main thoroughfare, yet he didn't miss the forlorn note in her voice. "For what?"

"For getting you into all this. It was too much to ask of you."

"If I remember right, you didn't twist my arm. I offered my services."

She lifted her head and looked at him. "Yes, but you couldn't have known that things were going to get so out of hand. I certainly didn't."

The only thing that had gotten out of hand was his heart, he thought. "Don't worry about me."

"But I do, Rick. And—and I've missed you this past week."

He darted her a glance. "Missed me? Darling, we've seen each other every day."

"I know. But we haven't had the chance to be together. Not like we always were before Mother and Tracie came to town."

Her words made Rick's insides go as soft as putty. He'd missed being with Priscilla, too, and all the simple things they did together. A meal, a shared cup of coffee before Priscilla went to bed, a quiet walk on the beach. Why, he hadn't even had a chance to get into her root beers this week.

"Tell you what, sugar. After your mother and sister go home we'll take a drive down the coast, take a picnic and swim. How does that sound?"

Her smile was warm, her eyes shining, as she reached over and lightly touched his arm. "You're the most wonderful friend I could ever have, Rick."

"I aim to please, darlin'," he said as cheerfully as he could manage, but inside he wondered if he'd ever walk on firm foundation again. Exactly what did he really want to be to Priscilla? he asked himself.

Chapter Ten

"Rick, what did you do, invite the whole typing pool?" Priscilla hissed under her breath.

She plastered a smile on her face and clung to Rick's arm as they entered the crowded room.

"I couldn't invite one woman and not the others," Rick whispered back. "Besides they were all dying to see you."

Priscilla had to stifle a groan as people began to throng around them.

"Here are the lovebirds," someone said.

"Fifteen minutes late. They must have stopped for a necking session," another person added in a loud voice.

Laughter spilled around them and someone shoved a glass of champagne each into their hands.

Priscilla sipped and smiled and tried her best to respond to the deluge of congratulations.

Eventually a combo began to play and couples began to flow out onto the dance floor. One of the teachers she worked with left the crowd and rushed up to her.

"Priscilla!" the young woman gasped. "Love has certainly done things to you. You look gorgeous." She turned her eye on Rick who was presently sharing a drink with his company CEO. "Wherever did you find him? All this time, I expected you and Williard to get together. That must seem hilarious to you now."

Priscilla glanced down at the pale liquid in her glass. "Why do you say that?"

"Why?" Lori's laughter trilled loudly. "Priscilla, you're so deadpan it kills me. Comparing Williard to Rick is like comparing a nag to a thoroughbred. Do you mind if I have a dance with him later?"

From the look in Lori's eyes it probably wouldn't have mattered if Priscilla had minded. "Just don't get too close," Priscilla told her in a coy voice. "I might get jealous."

"Oh, Priscilla, you lucky thing. Just look at the way he's looking at you. I'd kill for a man to look at me like that."

Priscilla shifted her gaze to Rick, who was standing only a few feet away. He was looking at

Priscilla, but she deciphered it as one of his Olivier looks. He was getting great at them, she silently agreed, and each one was breaking her heart.

"If you'll excuse me, Lori, I need to have a word with my mother." Priscilla pushed her way through the crowd to a long banquet table set up on the opposite side of the room. Her mother was standing at the head of it sharing an animated conversation with a friend who had flown down from Longview just to be here tonight.

"Mother, the place looks beautiful, and the music is great." She stood on tiptoe and kissed her mother's cheek, then looked over to Gloria's friend. "Hello, Helen, I'm so glad you could come tonight," she said. "It means a lot to Rick and myself."

Helen clasped Priscilla's hand between both of hers. "I was very happy to hear of your engagement, Priscilla, and when your mother called, I simply had to come. Gloria has just been giving me a glowing account of your young man. Of course, I won't give my opinion until I get a chance to talk with him," she added teasingly.

Priscilla smiled. "No, you mustn't get away without meeting Rick." Especially so you can go back home to Jefferson and spread the word about him, she added silently. Where would it all end? she wondered dismally.

Someone tapped her on the shoulder and she turned around to see Williard towering over her.

His black hair was plastered to one side of his head and his glasses had slid to the end of his sharp nose. For some reason Lori's remark came back to her. "Well, hello, Williard. I'm glad you could come tonight."

The tall, painfully thin man smiled self-consciously down at her. "Would you like an hors d'oeuvre? The ones with the bacon are great."

Williard had always been kind to Priscilla, and she wasn't one to forget a kindness. He was also sensitive, and she hated to turn him down and hurt his feelings. "Sure," she told him, offering him her elbow.

Across the room Rick spotted them out of the corner of his eye. Why, that twirp, he fumed inwardly, who did he think he was, taking over Priscilla that way? Didn't he know she was an engaged woman now?

"I think I'll go get a refill, Fred," he said quickly to his boss. He headed across the room toward the serving table.

"Oh, Rick, there you are," Tracie called, rushing up to him as he made his way through the crowd. "Don't you think it's time to dance with your future sister-in-law?"

"I haven't even danced with Priscilla yet," he said in an effort to put her off.

Tracie waved away his words, as if they were nothing, and grabbed his arm. "Oh, she's busy with Mr. Science right now. Besides, you can dance with her any ol' time after you're married."

Rick looked across the way to Priscilla. She was popping an hors d'oeuvre into her mouth while listening closely to Williard's conversation. Suddenly she laughed, making Rick's jaw tighten. Wasn't Priscilla remembering how the man ate the same boring cereal every morning? How he cleaned his bird cage promptly every Saturday morning?

Rick became aware that Tracie was tugging him out onto the dance floor and he was obliged to turn his attention to her.

Across the room, Priscilla watched Rick from the corner of her eye. Damn Tracie! Who did she think she was? This was her engagement party and Rick was her fiancé! At least for tonight.

"I suppose you'll be quitting your job after you get married," Williard commented between bites of food.

Gritting her teeth, Priscilla forced her attention back on Williard. "Why do you think that?"

Williard shrugged. "I heard your fiancé is a high-powered businessman for Petro Gulf. You probably won't need to work."

Strange that Priscilla had never thought of Rick as a high-powered businessman. But, then, Rick had always had the ability to leave his work at work. "He does have an important job. He markets petroleum. Both raw and refined. But I plan to keep on working. Rick thinks teachers make a great contribution to society." Which was true enough, she thought.

"I'm glad he at least appreciates you for what you are," Williard said.

Priscilla wondered what that was suppose to mean, but was afraid to ask.

"Priscilla, congratulations!"

Priscilla turned to see Gary, another teacher who'd been included on the invitation. Priscilla hadn't wanted to invite him, because he was the biggest flirt in the whole school and had just divorced his wife. But she hadn't been able to think of a polite way to exclude him.

"Thank you, Gary. I hope you're enjoying the party."

"Oh, I am. Especially seeing you in that dress. It looks like this engagement has transformed you in ways I never imagined."

His lecherous gaze traveled over her as if he were seeing her for the first time. Priscilla was thankful when Rick chose that moment to walk up on the three of them.

"Ready for a dance, darling?" He put his arm around Priscilla's shoulders and pressed a kiss on her cheek.

"I thought you'd forgotten all about me," she

said with a pout that would have rivaled any of Scarlett O'Hara's.

"And how could I do that when you're the most beautiful woman here?" he drawled, a dangerous light in his blue eyes as he looked down at her.

She let his remark slide and quickly introduced him to the two male teachers. After the men exchanged a few words, Rick purposefully led Priscilla onto the dance floor.

Priscilla's hand was quivering as she slipped it into Rick's and allowed him to pull her close.

"What are you doing?" he mouthed against her ear. "We've only been here a few minutes and you start flirting! You're going to blow this whole thing!"

Priscilla gasped audibly. "What am *I* doing? What did you think *you* were doing, dancing with Tracie? I'm the woman you're engaged to. You were supposed to dance the first dance with me!"

"I couldn't help it. Tracie waylaid me while I was on my way over to tear you away from Williard!" he gritted in a low voice only she could hear.

"I hardly needed saving from Williard. He merely fetched me a plate of hors d'oeuvres."

Rick had never been jealous in his life, but tonight the green-eyed monster was clawing at his insides and there didn't seem to be any way he could stop it. "Why did you even invite him, anyway?"

She reared her head back to give him a scathing glare. "How could you dare ask, when you invited not less than fifty of your girlfriends!"

His expression was suddenly one of exaggerated boredom. "If you started counting back before my kindergarten year, you couldn't come up with fifty women that I've dated."

"Hmmph!" Priscilla snorted. "You've had at least twenty-five since you've moved in with me."

"I didn't move in with you. I moved in beside you. There is a big difference," he pointed out.

Priscilla's teeth ground together. "The only difference is that we don't share a bed."

Well, he'd certainly like to take her out of here and do something about that right now! The thought had him nearly tripping over his feet, which in turn threw Priscilla even closer to his chest.

After steadying them both, he said huskily, "You're missing the whole point, Pris."

Suddenly she blinked, then pressed her cheek against the front of his jacket. "Oh, there is no point, Rick," she wailed. "This whole thing is just a delusion."

Rick could hear the hoarseness in her voice and knew she was close to tears. The idea that she might cry tore at him. He'd only seen her cry once, and that had been when she'd discovered that one of her pupils had been physically abused at home. She'd blamed herself for not seeing it earlier and doing something about it. No, Priscilla never shed crocodile tears. If she cried, it was because her heart was hurting.

He reached up and cradled the back of her head with his palms. Her hair was fine and silky to the touch and the exotic perfume that had sent his mind drifting earlier was doing its work again. "I don't want to hear another word of that sort. I don't want to hear fake, phony, delusion, pretense or whatever synonym might apply. Do you hear me, Priscilla?"

"But, Rick—"

"But nothing," he swiftly interrupted, cupping her cheeks and lifting her face up to his. "Tonight our engagement is real. I'm the man you're going to marry. You're going to be my wife. I'm going to be your husband. Tomorrow is soon enough to go back to calling it all a sham, but tonight we are betrothed to each other."

Her eyes glimmered with unshed tears. Rick was trying to make her feel better. He just didn't know it was too late for that.

Rick lowered his head toward her. Instinctively Priscilla stood on tiptoe. The kiss was warm and lingering. Neither one was aware that the dance floor was deserted except for the two of them.

They were quickly made aware of the fact as a spattering of applause broke out around them.

Rick lifted his head and smiled at Priscilla's bemused expression. "I think we've made believers of them," he whispered.

The party lasted well past midnight. Priscilla was exhausted by the time they arrived back at the beach house. After the three women said goodnight to Rick she was ready to fall into bed and sleep for a week.

"Priscilla, you don't want to go to bed now," her mother said after Priscilla had voiced her intentions. "Let's have a cup of hot chocolate to unwind first. Will you make it, Tracie, dear? You still seem full of energy." Gloria looked at her other daughter for an answer.

Any other time, Tracie would have been outraged at being asked to do a menial task, tonight she merely grumbled and headed toward the kitchen. Gloria sat on the couch and patted the cushion beside her. Priscilla complied with her mother's wishes and joined her on the couch.

"Did you enjoy the party?" Gloria asked.

Priscilla pushed her fingers through her hair and leaned back against the chintz cushions. She'd enjoyed being with Rick. But she'd hated deceiving a room full of people. "It was wonderful. I really don't know how to thank you."

Gloria laughed. "You're not supposed to thank me, Priscilla. Not for doing something I so enjoyed doing. I'm your mother, remember."

"Well, I for one never expected it. You spent so much money and worked so hard!" Priscilla felt so badly about it all. But she hadn't asked for the party. Her mother had virtually forced it on her, she told herself.

Gloria patted her daughter's knee. "Let's not worry about that. Your father and I have plenty to spend on you girls. Now I'm ready to get on to the big event. And since I'm leaving in the morning I thought it would be nice if we chatted about it tonight."

The big event. Did her mother mean what Priscilla was afraid she meant? One look at her mother's glowing face gave her the answer.

"Mother, how many times do I have to tell you. Rick and I haven't even set a date yet. It's far too early to think about wedding details."

Gloria waved away her words as if they were nothing. "If I'm betting right, Rick will be ready in a matter of days. And you know how men are— they don't know us women need to be forewarned. No, it's best I go ahead and have some of the arrangements already taken care of. That way everything will be ready when you do pick a date."

"But, Mother—" she began in an anxious tone.

Gloria's expression was suddenly stricken. "Oh,

Pris, you two don't plan to elope, do you? I mean, it would kill me if you deprived me of seeing you married. But if that's what you want—''

"Er, no, we don't plan on eloping. But—''

Gloria let out a relieved breath. "Thank goodness. Now about the church. I'll ask Pastor Wingate about it as soon as I get back home. You do want him to perform the ceremony, don't you? I know he wasn't the pastor there while you were growing up, but you do at least know him, and since Brother Reynolds has passed on, anyway, I don't really see any choice, do you?''

Priscilla's head was virtually swimming. "No. But Mother, what if—?'' Priscilla stopped, unable to finish with what if something happened and the engagement was broken. Her mother was happier than she'd seen her in a long time. Priscilla couldn't bring herself to hurt her. At least not tonight.

"What if what, baby? Would you prefer to have the ceremony at home? You know we could have it outside,'' Gloria went on in a thoughtful voice. "By next week your father's prize roses will be in full bloom. It would be a lovely setting.''

Next week! Priscilla felt close to panic. "Mother, next week is—''

"What about next week?'' Tracie questioned as she carried in the hot chocolate.

"I was just telling Priscilla that an outside wedding at home would be beautiful with your father's prize roses coming into bloom.''

"You're getting married next week?" Tracie asked as she passed around the mugs.

"Well, I don't know. Rick hasn't said—"

"Priscilla," Gloria interrupted once again, "if there's one thing I've learned about Rick, it's that he'll do anything to make you happy. If you want to get married next week, I'm sure he'll be all for it.''

Rick would do anything to make her happy, she repeated to herself. If only that were so. Her mother didn't realize that Rick put marriage in the same category as the bubonic plague.

"Prissy, you are going to ask me to be your maid of honor, aren't you? If you don't, I'll be absolutely furious with you," Tracie said.

Priscilla sipped the hot chocolate while watching her sister kick off her high heels and curl up in a chair. It was obvious that Tracie wasn't speaking sarcastically. Priscilla realized her sister now believed the engagement was a real one. And Tracie was actually beginning to treat her younger sister with a little more love and respect. For some insane reason, that made Priscilla feel even more like a fraud.

"I—there wouldn't be anyone else I would ask," she told Tracie, while wishing the floor would suddenly develop a hole and swallow her up.

"Oh, my goodness!" their mother exclaimed. "I've just thought of the garden-club ladies. I'm sure they'll insist on giving you a bridal shower. And then the VFW ladies won't want to be outdone and will probably give you one, too. You should be thinking about china patterns and a color scheme, so I can pass the information along...."

Two hours later, Priscilla tossed back and forth on her bed. So far she hadn't been able to shut her eyes, much less fall asleep. This whole thing was getting out of hand. It had already gotten that way. And what was it all going to prove? she asked herself. That she could make her mother and sister proud of her, if she pretended to be something she wasn't?

Priscilla did want to make her family happy and proud of her. But she couldn't do it like this. A lie can't live forever. Not only was it weighing her conscience down, but her mother was going to expect her and Rick to be in Jefferson next week for a wedding.

Throwing back the sheet, Priscilla tiptoed across the room. Thankfully the house was dark and her mother and sister were asleep in the spare bedroom. Once she reached the kitchen, Priscilla quietly turned the knob on the door leading into Rick's side of the house.

She had to talk to him tonight. Her mother was leaving in the morning. She couldn't let her go back home and start planning a wedding that was never going to take place.

Rick was obviously in bed, too. The house was quiet and dark. She tiptoed her way slowly through the familiar, but cluttered rooms, cursing under her breath as she came close to tripping over numerous unidentified objects.

"Rick! Are you awake?" she whispered when she finally entered his bedroom.

There was a groan and a shifting of the mattress. Priscilla squinted, as she tried to make out his form in the darkness.

"Priscilla, is that you?" he asked groggily.

"Yes. I've got to talk to you. Now!" She entered the room and immediately stubbed her toe on a barbell. "Damn it, Rick! A person could get killed in this house!"

He raised up on his elbow to see her hopping on one foot, while painfully clutching the other one. "I put that barbell in that specific spot because I knew you'd come sneaking in here at three o'clock in the morning," he said tersely.

She rubbed her toe a moment longer, then carefully approached the bed. "It couldn't be helped. Mother is out of control."

Rick reached up and switched on the bedside lamp. Priscilla sank onto the edge of the mattress.

"That's not news, Priscilla," he replied. He leaned back against the pillows, folding his hands behind his head. His eyes immediately went to her nightwear. She had on Mickey again, and his mouth twisted wryly at the sight of her in the long T-shirt. "Why do you insist on tormenting that mouse? He's an innocent little guy. He's never been faced with anything like that before."

Priscilla glared at him. "Rick! This is serious. I didn't walk through an obstacle course of booby traps just to discuss my state of dress or undress with you."

He immediately put on a serious expression, but a wicked twinkle was still in his blue eyes.

Priscilla was suddenly aware that Rick had nothing on. At least nothing above the waist. She didn't dare think what she might see below the waist.

He was a beautifully made male, tanned to a deep nut brown that made his blue eyes startling, especially since he was lying between blue sheets. But right now she was finding other things to look at besides his eyes. She'd often seen him in swimming trunks, but somehow seeing him in bed in an undressed condition seemed altogether different.

She swallowed and started again. "Mother is going home in the morning."

He gave her a bored look. "You came all the

way in here to give me a repeat of the ten-thirty news?''

"But that's not all, smartie. When she gets there, she's going straight to Pastor Wingate to make wedding arrangements. That's not to mention all the bridal showers that will probably be planned."

At this news, Rick sat straight up in the bed. Priscilla watched the blue sheet slide unheeded down his chest to stop a scandalous inch or two below his navel. As Priscilla suspected, he was obviously naked, and the idea left her flushed all over.

"The woman is out of control," he muttered.

Priscilla cut him a dreary glance. "Now who's doing the repeating?"

His expression became grim. "What are we going to do?"

"I'm going to—"

He snapped his fingers. "I know! I've got a doctor friend. I'll have him diagnose me with a contagious disease. We can't get married if I'm in quarantine."

Priscilla shook her head defeatedly. "I'm through with this whole thing, Rick."

"What?"

"You heard me. It's obvious that one lie calls for another. Now we've made up so many lies we don't even know where the truth begins and ends. I don't like it, and I can't do it anymore."

"Priscilla, snap out of it. Pull yourself together. We'll think of something to put her off. I'll simply tell her I'm not ready to get married."

Priscilla rubbed her fingers across her forehead. "I've already tried that. She thinks you'll be ready to do anything to make me happy." Priscilla looked at him from the corner of her eye. "You were even better than Olivier, Rick. She truly believes you're madly in love with me."

Well, he was, wasn't he? he asked himself. No! He couldn't be. All those years ago he'd vowed to avoid the pain of love. But what had it meant tonight at the party, when he'd felt like killing every man who had touched Priscilla? Was it love, just because she was the woman he wanted to find waiting for him when he came home from work? Was it love, because he found her funnier, warmer, sweeter than any other woman he'd ever known? No. It couldn't be, he silently argued with himself.

"That's what we were wanting, wasn't it?" he asked softly.

"Well, yes. But not to this extent! At this rate she'll expect us to have a child in six months!"

"That's not possible," he said, then one brow raised at Priscilla. "Or does she think that we—?"

Priscilla rolled her eyes. "Rick, I do know about sex and babies! I was merely trying to get my point over. Of course Mother doesn't think we've been sleeping together!''

That was ironic, Rick thought. He'd been thinking about them sleeping together virtually night and day.

Priscilla began to twist her fingers nervously together. Rick reached over and covered them with his own hand.

"Priscilla, I know you're worried. But that doesn't mean we have to spill the beans now, after all we've been through.''

His hand was warm and comforting, Priscilla's fingers instinctively clutched it with hers. "Rick, I know that I'm the one who started this whole mess. I'll even concede that it was you who tried to talk me out of it in the first place.'' She took a deep breath then slowly released it. "And I admit now that I should have listened to you. I should have immediately called my mother back and set her straight on the matter. I should have told her that Tracie had started the whole lie. At least we wouldn't have wound up in this horrid situation.''

Rick felt his heart begin to melt at the quiver in her voice. "You didn't want to let your mother down. And you haven't. In my opinion, she couldn't be happier.''

Priscilla grimaced. "She's happy because she thinks I'm something I'm not.''

"That's nonsense. She's happy because she believes you're getting married, that you're starting out on a happy life with me.''

Priscilla looked at him and laughed, but there was more sting in it than humor. ''Wouldn't she find it hilarious to discover you're Galveston's best-known playboy?''

''Now, Pris, that's hardly fair.''

Priscilla shook her head and waved away her words. ''Oh, I know,'' she said contritely. ''It's not your fault that you like women. It's not my fault that I'm boring and conventional. But it is the truth. And it's high time Mother finally knew it.''

An unexplained panic swiftly rushed through Rick and he gripped her hand. ''Okay, go ahead and tell her that I like women and you're boring. I mean,'' he quickly stammered with frustration, ''you're not boring, but that you like to be in bed by ten o'clock. That's enough of a confession.''

''Rick, you don't understand. I've learned something from this whole farce, and that is the most important thing after all is to simply be yourself. I can't be something I'm not, just to make my parents or sister think more highly of me. They or anyone else will simply have to take me as I am. I believe I am worthy of some man's love, and someday I'll find him. But right now I've got to tell Mother our engagement has all just been pretend.''

Rick was virtually motionless as he stared at her

face. This was his Priscilla talking, and it was killing him to hear her say that their engagement didn't really mean anything.

"You can't do that," he blurted out.

Chapter Eleven

"Why?" Priscilla asked.

"Well, because," he quickly reasoned. "We've put too much into this. And think of all the pain and disappointment you're going to put your mother through."

Sighing, Priscilla rose from the bed. "Yes, I know. And I feel terrible about it. But someday, when I do really get married, it will make up for this."

Closing his eyes, Rick raked his hands through his hair. He would make an awful husband, wouldn't he? He was messy and bossy, and he liked to stay up late, eat in bed and watch TV. Priscilla hated all that. She wanted someone who was organized and conventional, someone who read Yeats. "Priscilla, I—don't you think we could pretend a little longer?"

She turned her head to look at him over her shoulder. "What in the world for? I imagine you're ready to get on with your life. And I know I certainly am ready to get on with mine." She also knew she couldn't survive more pretending. She loved Rick too much to pretend she didn't. Now she was going to have to work at getting over him, and she certainly couldn't do that with him hanging around like a loving fiancé.

"But I'm just now getting good at it."

She came back and sat down on the edge of the bed. "Poor thing, all that champagne you drank tonight must have given you delusions of an acting career." She laid her hand on his brow. "Are you feeling all right?"

Actually he was feeling crazy and reckless, and very much in love. "I don't know," he said quietly. "You tell me. You seem to have all the answers tonight."

Priscilla looked down at her hands lying loosely in her lap to see the engagement ring winking up at her. It instantly reminded her of the night he'd given it to her, and all the trouble he'd taken to make it seem like the real occasion. She'd loved him then. Looking back on it now, she must have always loved him.

Tears scalded the back of her eyes as she removed it and handed it over to him. But she fiercely blinked them back before he had a chance to see them. "You never did tell me what the ring cost. I'll give you the money for it tomorrow," she said quietly.

"I really doubt it," he said. "It would take several of your paychecks."

She looked up at him, confusion marring her face. "What?"

Solemnly he held the diamond up between his thumb and forefinger. "I said you couldn't pay me for it. At least not pay me and pay your rent, too."

Priscilla suddenly gasped. "Are you trying to tell me that the ring you're holding is a real diamond? It's too big to be real!"

Rick reached for her hand and pushed the ring back on her finger. "A woman worthy of a man's love is worthy of a real ring, don't you think?"

Priscilla laughed, as though she wasn't quite sure which one of them had lost their mind. "Rick, this is not a time for teasing! I told you to buy a cubic zirconia. And that's what you bought. A fake. Isn't it?" she asked, her voice suddenly doubtful.

Lifting her hand for a closer inspection, she

squinted closely at the stone. This past week she'd looked at it over and over, and at times she'd thought it so beautiful it had to be real. But then she'd told herself she'd only been wishing it so strongly in her mind that she was only imagining things. After all, it was beautiful simply because Rick had given it to her.

As Rick watched an array of emotions cross her precious face, he knew he couldn't go on fighting his feelings. His parents had lived out a terrible marriage and their unhappiness had scared him away from love and marriage. But now, thinking of life without Priscilla was the thing that scared him the most.

He reached for her shoulders and twisted her down against the mattress. "The ring is real and so is this," he murmured, lowering his head down to her.

Dazed, Priscilla watched his lips grow closer and closer. "Rick, what are—?"

Her question was quickly blotted out as he moved his mouth over hers. Priscilla didn't know what was happening except that Rick was kissing her, and she wanted so very much to kiss him back. Mindlessly, her arms moved up and around his bare back.

They were both breathless by the time Rick broke away, leaning back just enough to look into her eyes. "I'm trying to tell you that I love you, that I want you to be my wife."

Priscilla pushed at his shoulders. "Rick, don't tell me that. You know you don't want to get married. You hate the whole idea!"

Groaning, he shook his head, then reached up and stroked the stray hair from her forehead. "I hate the idea of not having you in my life. I hate to think of you with any other man but me."

Rick watched her eyes fill with wonder and his heart began to trip against his ribs. "Pris, I know you're my friend, but could you be more than that?"

Rick was saying he wanted to marry her. It was practically too much for Priscilla to take in. "Rick, when I tried to talk to you about marriage, you— And all those girlfriends—"

"Priscilla," he cut in before she could continue, "I've always told myself I'd never let myself fall in love or get married. For years, all I could see was my parents fighting and making each other miserable. Their marriage was a disaster. I didn't want that kind of life for myself. And now I can see that I purposely dated women I knew were wrong for me."

Priscilla scanned his face with serious eyes. "And you think we're right for each other, that we wouldn't make each other miserable?"

A slow smile spread across his face and Priscilla's heart turned over at the depth of love in his eyes. What she saw couldn't be an act.

"I think we'd be miserable if we weren't together. This past week has shown me just how much you mean to me. It's also taught me that falling in love is something you have no control over."

"I thought this week had driven you crazy," she said.

His smile was tender as he softly stroked her cheek and the freckles across her nose. "It has. Do you know how frustrating it is to be in love with someone and have to pretend that you're only pretending to be in love with her?"

Priscilla giggled. "Can you run that by me again?"

He chuckled, then lowered himself against her, resting both his elbows on either side of her head. "Do you love me?"

She dimpled wryly. "Are you sure that diamond is real?"

He moved his mouth to within a tantalizing fraction of hers. "Very sure. Now do you love me?"

Her lips brushed his as they moved into a wide smile. "You idiot," she gently whispered, "I've loved you for a long time. Don't you know I wouldn't cook my special meatballs for anyone I didn't love.''

"You didn't know you loved me," he accused.

"You didn't know you loved me," she countered.

"You wanted to find me a good woman," he reminded her.

"Yes, but the only one I could think of was me," she confessed.

"Isn't that a coincidence? The only man I could think of perfect enough for you was me."

He kissed her. Then Priscilla asked, "What about Mother's wedding plans? She wants us to be married in Daddy's rose garden."

With a husky laugh he rolled to his back and pulled Priscilla over on top of him. "Tell her we'll be there."

Priscilla's expression was very serious as she cradled his face with her hands. Rick had taught her so much. About love. And about herself. She knew now that she was just as special in her own right as the next person. And Rick was more than a precious pretender to her. He was her very heart, and the thing she wanted most was for him to be happy and sure of their love. "This time it won't be pretend, Rick. It will be the real thing."

"The real thing," he repeated softly, his eyes warm with love. "That's what I want with you, sugar.'' His hands circled her waist, then slid possessively up her back to draw her closer to him. ''Just tell me one thing, Priscilla,'' he said, glancing down at her nightshirt. ''That mouse won't come between us after we're married, will he?''

She laughed and lowered his head to kiss him. ''Nothing will ever come between us, my dearest Rick. This is the real thing.''

* * * * *

Silhouette®

SPECIAL EDITION™

Emotional, compelling stories that
capture the intensity of living,
loving and creating a family
in today's world.

Silhouette®

Desire.

A highly passionate,
emotionally powerful and
always provocative
read.

Silhouette®

Silhouette®

Where love comes alive™

Silhouette®

INTIMATE MOMENTS™

A roller-coaster read that delivers
romantic thrills in a world of
suspense, adventure
and more.

Silhouette *Romance*

From first love to forever,
these love stories are for
today's woman with
traditional values.

Where love comes alive™

From first love to forever, these love stories are
for today's woman with traditional values.

A highly passionate, emotionally powerful
and always provocative read.

SPECIAL EDITION™

Emotional, compelling stories that capture the
intensity of living, loving and creating a family in
today's world.

Silhouette

INTIMATE MOMENTS™

A roller-coaster read that delivers romantic thrills
in a world of suspense, adventure and more.

Escape to a place where a kiss is still a kiss...
Feel the breathless connection...
Fall in love as though it were
the very first time...
Experience the power of love!

Come to where favorite authors—such as
Diana Palmer, Stella Bagwell,
Marie Ferrarella and many more—
deliver heart-warming romance and genuine
emotion, time after time after time....

Silhouette Romance—
stories straight from the heart!